Collateral DAMAGE

L♥VE & DECEPTION

A NOVEL

DON HENDRIXX

Swagg Motivation 101 Publishing

In honor of your greatness, this is not a farewell but a heartfelt dedication:

To my beloved sister, Jasmine Mae Shields, may you forever be my Guardian Angel, illuminating even the darkest moments of my life. I hold firm in my belief that our Lord and Savior watches over you with utmost care. September 4, 1995 – October 11, 2004.

To my cousin, Willie Hubbard-McGee, known as Tray, the talented Quarterback of the Trinity Trojans, I express my gratitude for the time we shared. Your presence was an inspiration, and you remain one of the most exceptional high school quarterbacks I have witnessed. October 19, 1991 – April 14, 2017.

To my dear grandmother, Ulia Curry McGee, your departure leaves me in disbelief. Words fail to convey the depth of my emotions, but I take solace in being a part of your bloodline. I find joy in knowing that your pain has ceased. May the legacy of the legendary Ulia Curry McGee endure. November 22, 1931 – February 13, 2018

To my father, Victor Hill, I want to express how deeply I miss you. Your presence has been a constant inspiration throughout my life. I am well aware of the love you had for me. You entrusted me with the care of our mother, and I assure you, I still watch over her. I love you, Dad. May the memory of one of the greatest men in my life endure. May 18, 1961 – February 21, 2023

To my Aunt Darlene, her laughter, warmth, and wisdom will forever resonate within us. Her love for family and knack for finding beauty in every moment defined her. As we bid farewell, we embrace the lessons she imparted and treasure the memories she left us. Rest in peace, beloved Aunt Darlene. You will be greatly missed and forever cherished. March 14, 1969- July 24, 2023

Contents

Collateral Damage: Love & Deception "Poem"

L ove, a fragile rose, so delicate and sweet,
    It blooms in hearts, a rare and precious treat.
But often, like a wild storm, it roars,
And leaves behind the wreckage of shattered hearts.

Deception, a viper's venom, poisonous and sly,
It takes hold of trust and buries it deep inside.
It deceives the heart, with lies and half-truths told,
And leaves behind a trail of broken dreams, so cold.

Collateral Damage, the aftermath of love gone wrong,
It's the innocent victims left to suffer, all along.
In the aftermath of battles fought, and lost,
The shards of love that remain, the cost.

But amidst the ruins of love and deception's game,
There lies a shimmering thread, that glitters like a flame.
Its hope, a fiery glow, that brightens in the dark,
The glue that holds the broken pieces of love's arc.

Let us tread lightly with love, as if caressing a delicate rose,
And hold it close, whatever life may expose.
Let trust be the anchor, that keeps love's melody near,
And leave behind the sting of deception's fear.

For love is a rare and precious thing, a treasure to behold,
It fills hearts with joy, like a rare and precious gold.
And though the cost may sometimes be high,
It's worth it, for love is priceless, and it will never die.

Chapter 1

Passions, Promises and Uncertain Paths

I sat in the den, on the couch, watching a movie with my baby. After a while, I picked up the Star-Telegram newspaper. What I saw both surprised and irritated the hell out of me. There I was on the front page, the words "Notorious Drug Lord on the Rise" written right underneath my picture. *Society finally got wind of my secret organization.* I stood up abruptly and began to pace, devouring the words as I did.

As I continued to read, Mayor Young's words leaped out from the page at me. "The M.O.B Crime Family is a threat to society, so we as a people need to bring them down for good. The killing needs to stop! I came to bring justice &

peace to our society."

How the fuck can that ole Sambo ass nigga talk. He is more crooked than most of the criminals in this city. The thought of it all hurt my stomach as my hands squeezed around the newspaper.

I began to wonder where the hell he was getting most of his information from because 75% of it was valid, but the other 25% was a straight-up lie. I came a long way from not having shit, so he got me fucked up if he thought I was just gon' to let him fuck up my business. Talking about getting justice, is that nigga crazy? It's time to get rid of that nigga for good.

"Knock, knock." I heard the voice, accompanied by a tap on the door.

"Who is it?" I screamed. I was still furious from the bullshit I had just read.

"May I come in to holler at you for a second?" the voice said behind the door.

Please, God, I hope it isn't more bad news because I have had enough of that shit for one day. If I hear any more, I may just flip the fuck out. "Come on in; the door is un-locked." I hollered.

My right-hand man, D-Black, came in and said, "King, me and the boys are about to head to Crab Shack over there in the Highlands. Do you and Queenie want to come?"

I wasn't in the mood to eat, so I passed, but turned to

my baby and asked, "Do you want anything?"

"No, thank you. I just want some alone time with King," she responded with a naughty grin on her face. That made me grin as a million sexual fantasies passed through my head.

"Where is Sergio? Because I haven't seen him all day,' I asked D-Black.

"Sergio is at some thot's house, and he will be back in the morning," D-Black responded.

I didn't trip because I already knew how my brother was. I just hoped that he would stay out of trouble because trouble always seemed to find him. I told D-Black, "Whenever you talk to him again, tell him I said to get at me ASAP. We have some business to discuss.

"Ok, Boss, I will get on top of that as soon as I hear from him. Do you want any of the boys to stand watch outside the house?"

I needed my alone time with my baby, so I turned the extra help down. I also wanted my boys to enjoy themselves. They needed as much rest as the work they had put in. "Enjoy yourselves but watch your backs and don't get too comfortable. There is no telling who might be lurking. We do not need to be going to war with no one right now. We have too much other shit to be worried about."

"Ok, boss." He nodded and then paused as though he had a second thought. "You sure you don't want anyone to stand watch because I don't want you and your girl here without protection, boss. I would feel horrible if something happened to you all."

I knew that was coming. This nigga pulls this shit every time just so he can see me act a fool. He didn't know how irritated I was. I hollered, "No damn, I don't need anyone watching over us tonight, and I know how to defend myself!"

D-Black grinned at me and said, "My bad boss," as he walked out of my room.

That's my boy. We have been through so much shit together, and he always had my back throughout the storm."

After my boys took off, it was just me and my baby, India.

"What would you like to do with our alone time?" I asked, looking at India with lust in my eyes."

She bit on her bottom lip teasingly. "I don't know, bae, You are the man in this relationship, and it is your job to take care of all the small details." She gave me a deep kiss on the lips.

That's when it dawned upon me that it had been a couple of months since we had any real alone time together.

"I am so sorry for neglecting you for so long," I said.

"I forgive you," she replied, with a slight smile lurking by the corners of her mouth and a pointed look in her eyes. "You and I both know what has kept you away from me."

She was right. It was my organization that took up most of my time. I knew India wanted me to give it up and go legit, but I couldn't make a promise I might break in the future.

I looked into her eyes and said, "Baby, I already know what you want, but it's hard dropping the ball right now since I've been tied to it for so long. This isn't something I can push to the side overnight."

India had mentioned that she wanted me to start my own record label or something like that. That way, I could make some money and keep the feds and police off my back. It was a good idea, but at this moment, not a practical one. Now she looked at me with doubtful eyes.

"I lied when I promised that I would get out, but don't worry, I will get out of the dope game as soon as I have made enough money for us to live a comfortable life," I promised her.

"This wouldn't be the first time you have said this to me. You told that lie several times before." She began to cry.

I knew she was afraid to lose me to all the violence that came with being a player in this dope game, especially a high-profile cat such as me.

"I am hungry." I tried to change the subject because I hated seeing her upset.

"You have to make a choice, honey," she said. "I will walk away before I visit you behind bars or at a gravesite."

I brushed it off. "What would you like to eat?" I asked again.

"Surprise me—and I meant every word," she replied

with a firm gaze.

The perfect dish for me came to me at that moment.

"I'll be right back with something delightful," I said.

I must say I am a beast in that kitchen when it comes to cooking dope or food. I went into the kitchen, pulled some Maine lobster out of the fridge, and put it in the oven to cook. I pilled two plates with some artichoke salad and two small plates with a slice of Goya mango pineapple pie which is her favorite dessert. I called this my *Ala shi mi* extraordinary. I also grabbed a bottle of her favorite red wine. After the lobster was done, I walked into the den, where my baby had lit some Champagne toast scented candles from Bath and Body Works. I sat the feast down on a red picnic blanket.

After we ate, I told her she should slip into something more comfortable. Imagine my surprise when she came in with a red negligee and some red bottoms on. I instantly got rock hard.

However, I had to set the moment right. "Hey, Alexa, play Chris Brown Under the Influence," I said.

As the music filtered into the room, India started to dance sensuously around me. She locked me in a passionate gaze, her body twirling to the rhythm. I got up and went back to the kitchen. I came out with a can of whipped cream and grabbed my baby. I carried her in my arms into the bedroom while she squirmed and laughed, telling me to put her down.

"You are not going anywhere until I am done satisfying every inch of your body," I said as I laid her down on the bed.

"You are the most wonderful man I ever met and I cannot wait to be your wife." She gazed into my eyes, twisting the big rock on her finger. Then she said the words I was waiting to hear. "Come, get it, Daddy."

I love India. She is my world, although we have had so many trials and errors with one another. My only wish was to make her happy for the rest of our lives. I prayed that our beautiful lives would not be cut short because of my lifestyle.

Hovering over her tantalizing body, I started kissing India, nice and slow. I slipped my tongue into her mouth and nibbled on her bottom lip. I planted wet kisses all over her beautiful face. When I made my way to her neck, I could hear her sigh in anticipation of what was to come.

"Baby, my pussy is wet; I need you...now!"

That's when I knew it was time to get down to business. I took the whipped cream and covered both of her nipples with it. I started sucking on her nipples lightly. She moaned and gasped as I stuck two fingers inside her. I opened up her pussy lips wide and placed my tongue right on her clit, sucking and licking in unison. All the while, I had my fingers inside her juicy flower. The faster I thrust my fingers and sucked on her clit, the more out of control, she got.

"Don't stop," screamed India. "Yes, King, this is all yours," as she bucked wildly in bed.

"Ride my face; let me taste every inch of this body," I said. At that point, she started to squirt, damn near drowning my ass, but you better believe I drank every drop.

Her legs were trembling at that point, but that didn't stop her from grabbing the whipped cream and covering my pipe with it. She started at the base and proceeded to lick me like an ice cream cone.

"Who does this dick belong to?" asked India, slurping on every inch of my manhood.

"Queenie!" I replied.

She took both of my balls in her mouth, licking and cleaning every drop of whipped cream off me. That shit felt extremely good! She took it to the next level when she started sucking me quickly. As soon as I felt that nut building up at the base of my spine, she jumped up in a doggy-style position.

"Fuck me this way baby," she said.

"Your wish is my command," I said as I began to pound the hell out of that pussy. Her wall was so tight and inviting. She was screaming that I was hitting her G-spot. I knew I had her ass then. She started squirting like a faucet at that point, and I could not hold back any longer as I exploded deep within her. She looked at me with anger in her eyes.

"What did I tell you about busting a nut inside me?" she asked, her eyes blazing hot.

"I don't care what you said; I couldn't help it," I replied.

She knew I wanted her to have my baby, but for some reason, she was not on board with that plan yet. I know it must be about my lifestyle, but I did not care because I wanted a mini-me to raise and love.

After that first round, we just laid there holding one another. I knew we were in for a long night. I got rock hard again, and she made sure I stayed that way. We took turns making each other explode for the rest of the night. At about five in the morning, she got up and proceeded to the shower. You know I was right behind her. The sway of them hips and that ass would have any nigga gladly following her to the ends of the earth. We took turns, washing each other, and then we crawled into our king-size bed pulled the duvet back over us, and drifted off to sleep, bathed in the glow of the rising sun.

Chapter 2

Crossroads of The Hearts

When I woke up, my eyes immediately darted to the clock. It was already a quarter to seven, signaling that I was running dangerously late for work. The thought of being stuck in that dreadful job for another day intensified my desire to quit. King, my boyfriend, had permitted me to leave, but with his risky lifestyle, I felt more secure having a second source of income. Besides, I enjoyed being independent and taking care of myself.

My baby was peacefully sleeping, and I didn't want to disturb him. So, I gently kissed his cheek and left a note expressing my love for him. I rushed to get dressed, ready to face the day ahead. Just as I was about to leave, my iPhone buzzed incessantly. It was an unusual time for someone to call me, considering everyone knew my work schedule. I glanced at the screen, and my heart skipped a beat. It was my ex-fiancé's phone number displayed across the screen.

"I don't have time for his bullshit," I thought, ignoring his calls. I had just spent a beautiful night with the love of my life, and I refused to let my ex ruin my good mood. I tucked the phone away and hurried out the door.

As I sped down the highway, a sense of panic washed over me as I noticed flashing police lights behind me. I pulled over to the side of the road upon hearing the blaring sirens. My mind raced with thoughts of the impending speeding ticket and the fact that I would undoubtedly be late for work.

When I saw the approaching figure through the window, my jaw dropped. It was my ex-fiancé, who also happened to be a cop. "Not today," I muttered under my breath.

"What's the problem, officer?" I asked, trying to maintain composure.

"India, please listen to me. I'm sorry for all the trouble I've caused you," pleaded Tyrone, my ex. "I couldn't help but see you. You're my world, and I want us to get back together."

This guy is delusional, I thought to myself, suppressing my anger and keeping quiet.

"I know you've been receiving my calls and messages, India," he continued. "Baby, please just talk to me. I know you're still with that criminal, King Dreadz, or whatever he calls himself. You deserve better."

I couldn't hold back any longer. "Deserve better, huh?" I blurted out. "That's quite amusing coming from you."

"I am a grown-ass woman, and I choose who I want to be with," I asserted. "You no longer have any control over me. I don't associate with shady individuals like you anymore, so move on with your life."

Tyrone looked into my eyes, his expression filled with regret. "I am truly sorry for my actions. I treated you poorly, and I regret it deeply. If I could go back and change things, I would."

His words stirred up emotions within me, and tears welled up in my eyes. Despite everything, I realized I still had some lingering feelings for him.

"To be together again, I need you to cut ties with King," Tyrone said, making a complex request.

It was a challenging proposition, and I wasn't prepared for such a demand.

"What are you going to do about all this love that we have for one another?" Tyrone asked.

"Nothing at all," I replied firmly. "But I will consider the possibility of us reconciling." I couldn't fathom why this guy had such power over me. He had already made a fool out of me twice, yet here I was, entertaining the idea of giving him another chance.

Tyrone chuckled and took out his ticket pad. "I'm sorry.

Things will be different this time, but I still have to write you a ticket since the dash cam is on," he explained.

I seethed with frustration, realizing I was not only dealing with emotional turmoil but also the consequences of being late for work.

Finally, I arrived at my workplace, and to my dismay, my boss was waiting at the front door, clearly livid.

"This is the last time you'll be late. The next instance will be your last because I'll have you fired," he threatened through clenched teeth.

I wanted to give him a piece of my mind and walk out, but I held my composure. He knew how much he needed me, so I dismissed his empty threats.

On my way to the break room, I spotted my best friend, Irene. I greeted her with my usual enthusiasm, and she responded with a warm hug. That's what I cherished about our friendship — mutual respect and support built over the years.

"Stop by my office when you have a moment. There's something I want to discuss," I said to her.

Without hesitation, Irene grabbed her cup of coffee and joined me in my office. She had an uncanny ability to sense when something was bothering me.

Behind closed doors, her first words were, "What's wrong, bitch?" accompanied by a mischievous smirk. I proceeded to recount my encounter with Tyrone that morning. Irene despised him, having witnessed all the drama and pain he caused me, so she wasn't thrilled about me considering a reunion.

"Girl, you know Tyrone ain't no damn good," Irene said, infuriated. "I told you to stay away from that sorry excuse for a man. Remember when he cheated on you with your cousin?"

I could see the anger in her eyes, still vividly recalling that painful chapter.

"Luckily for him, it wasn't me he cheated on," Irene exclaimed. "If it were, I would have given him and that other woman a piece of my mind."

I remembered that painful betrayal all too well, yet I couldn't shake the lingering feelings I had for Tyrone. Perhaps he had genuinely changed.

"What do you plan on doing about this situation, Irene asked?" with a concerned look on her face.

"I honestly don't have an answer," I replied honestly. "I do love Kent'e, even though he's not around much, leaving me feeling lonely. But Tyrone was my first true love."

Irene shook her head. "I wish you would think it through before making a reckless decision," she advised. "I don't want to see you hurt anymore. Besides, I think Mr. Dreadz is a better match for you."

At that point, I didn't want to discuss it further. "Let's get back to work before we both get in trouble for slacking off," I suggested.

Irene agreed but not without leaving me with some final

words. "Just weigh your options before making a foolish mistake," she said, exiting the office.

That day, I couldn't escape the whirlwind of thoughts racing through my mind. During lunch break, I met up with Irene again and vividly described the events between me and Kent'e the previous night. I blushed as we reached the more intimate details.

Irene grinned mischievously. "Damn, girl, you two are wild," she remarked. "I need to find a man like that. Does Kent'e have a brother, cousin, or any available friends?"

"He does have a younger brother named Sergio," I revealed. "He needs a woman who can tame his wild nature."

Sergio and Kent'e were like night and day, their differences were evident even when they stood together. Nevertheless, Sergio exuded a captivating charm. He possessed unshakable confidence and an adventurous spirit.

I knew he had significant wealth and no one to share it with, always donning the finest attire and driving cars yet to hit the market.

"Can you arrange a meeting for me? I'd love to meet that untamed King," Irene said, her smile widening. "Maybe my good 'pussy' will tame him." We both erupted in laughter at her bold statement.

"Yeah, I think I can arrange that," I replied, considering Irene's preference for adventurous men with means. Perhaps she could be the one to bring out the best in Sergio. After finishing our gossip session about Kent'e and his brother, we vented about the state of the world. As our lunch break came to an end, it was time to return to our workstations.

After enduring the exhausting workday, I decided to give Tyrone a call.

"Hello, beautiful. How are you?" Tyrone greeted me warmly.

"I'm doing well. I've been thinking, and I believe we need to have a face-to-face conversation," I replied.

"Sure, you can come over," he suggested.

He provided his address, and for a brief moment, I hesitated. I wasn't entirely certain if I wanted to go through with this, but I mustered the courage and resolved to find out what awaited me.

Chapter 3

Deadly Business Dealings

B EEP, BEEP, BEEP my alarm sounded. I threw the motherfucker across the room. I hated that damn alarm sound.

"It" so fucking annoying," I mumble to myself. I looked over and noticed that India was gone, but in her place was a note. I flipped it open and read.

I had so much fun last night, and I have never felt that way in a long time.

I love you so much and am so sorry I didn't wake you up when I was leaving.

You looked so peaceful while you slept and I didn't have the heart to wake you, but I did give you a kiss. Xoxo.

Damn, I woke up with a hard-ass dick and couldn't even

get no good morning sex. Well, maybe next time. I knew my baby wanted to make her money, so I wasn't going to hate on her for leaving. I just wished she would quit so I could have her to myself as often as I wanted to. I could give my baby anything she needed and then some. I make her salary for the month in two days. Well, it was her choice, so I was not complaining about it. *Time to get up and get dressed so I can get to this money.*

After I finished getting ready, I called up the crew to discuss what this new day would bring. The first ones in the meeting room were Sergio and Ki, my beloved brother and sister. A couple of minutes later, everyone else followed suit.

"I have called this meeting to discuss new shipment arrangements," I said and watched as they looked at each other, wondering why we needed new shipment arrangements.

"This is because, our main connection, Yun-Wun, is on vacation and would not be back for a couple of months. Danny, one of ours, made a new Jamaican connection, so we would be going with that," I continued.

"So, I am letting you know so you can tell me what you think about our new arrangement," I said.

"I don't trust them Jamaicans," Peanut said.

"If the Jamaican cockroaches make one wrong move, then we would finish them up in one swoop," said Sergio, my crazy-ass brother. He then held up his AK-47 to demonstrate.

To loosen the tension in the room, my sister Ki said, "Why are you always looking for trouble Sergio, mama should have made trouble your middle name, since your ass is always in trouble."

He laughed and said, "Fuck you, sis."

"How much weight are we looking at?" asked D-Black.

"It's about twenty keys of black tar, fifty keys of pearl, and one hundred pounds of that Ganja," I informed everyone.

"This is one of our biggest shipments ever. We were just used to getting one or two keys a month, but this shipment right here could change our lives and put us on easy street for a long time," I continued.

Gino and Ki weren't paying attention to anything I was saying, because they were too busy smiling at each other like two love birds. They were too busy playing footsie under the table. I always tell family never to mix business with pleasure, but you can't tell grown motherfucker's shit. I cleared my throat to get Gino and Ki's attention.

"I hope everyone is paying attention because this is some serious shit right here. We need to stay focused on this mission because we never worked with these people before, so we need to keep our ears and eyes on the streets, just in case there is any funny business," I said, my eyes focused on the two.

After the meeting, I left a note for Gramps letting him

know that I would be home later and to tell India that if she came home. On my way out the door, I damn near forgot to call up my nigga Billy Ray to let him know we were on our way to his famous chop shop in Fort Worth. We rode three cars deep, looking like a family of mobsters. When we got to the shop, I got a feeling of nostalgia.

These old cats never change a damn thing, do they? I thought. I rang the bell, remembering to look into the camera so he could see my face.

At first, there was no answer, which I thought was odd seeing as I had just finished talking to him. Then after a few seconds, the gate opens, and out walks Billy Ray laughing his ass off. We gave each other a handshake and a hug. That nigga was so big he damn near picked me up off the ground. I didn't know how much I missed him until that very moment. We chit-chatted for a few minutes, and then we got down to business.

"So, what brings you my way, youngster?" Billy Ray asked.

"I'm in need of some guns and transportation," I said.

"Follow me, I just got some brand-new shit in," he replied, getting up and leading the way.

As we went through the noisy warehouse, I saw that he had all his workers working their asses off. We walked into a backroom where he kept all his merchandise. I knew this nigga wasn't bullshitting around. He had everything from M16 rifles to 22-caliber pistols.

"What do you have in mind?" he asked.

"Everything," I replied.

"Damn, you must have a real big shipment coming in or you're about to go to war with someone."

"Damn Unc, you know about our don't ask, don't tell policy," I said. The less he knew the better.

He smiled because he knew I was trying to protect him as well, so he didn't push the issue. If the feds or boys in blue ever come around asking questions, he didn't have one fucking answer and that's the way I wanted it to stay. I would never put another man in my business.

"You know I have love for you nephew so I'm not going to tax your ass. Give me 20 stacks and you can leave here with what you came for. We got a deal?" Billy Ray said.

"That's a deal Unc I'm a lookout for you," I replied, and we shook on it.

"D-Black go get the dough," I said to my man.

When he brought the cash, we counted out twenty racks and I even tipped five more for doing service with me.

When all the supplies were ready, I called in the crew to take the artillery to the three parked white vans out front.

"Make it back to me safe, nephew," Billy Ray said to me. He told me to leave my cars parked in the warehouse until our mission was finished. "No one would ever come looking for them here."

No one except my soldiers knew that Billy Ray and I were associated with each other. And that was just the way we liked it. As I walked away, I heard Billy say that it was a pleasure seeing me again. I looked back at him and said, "Same to you, old friend," and once again walked away with nothing but the upcoming mission on my mind.

We finally made it to the abandoned warehouse that the Jamaican Mafia owned in Dallas. There were a couple of other rundown buildings surrounding the warehouse. This area looked like the slums of an old horror flick, "The Return of The Living Dead" to be exact. I started canvassing the area to make sure nothing seemed suspicious or out of place. I instructed my crew to do the same.

The first people I noticed were the four heavily armed Jamaicans. They were standing next to a couple of parked cars. When I saw this, I rounded my crew up for a quick game plan meeting. I took Gino, D-Black, Tu Tank, and Black Mexican. I told the other ones to be waiting outside just in case some funny shit popped off. I, my crew, and my suitcase full of money headed towards our destination.

As we headed inside, I just happened to glance up and noticed out of the corner of my eye at least twenty Jamaicans posted on the roof with high-powered rifles. At that point, all my senses went on full alert. At that point, I wondered what exactly I had gotten myself into. I walked up to the leader or who I believed was the leader. He was 5'4 and about 250 pounds.

His dreads hung very low, and you could smell the Kush floating off of his clothing. He was smoking some of that good.

"I hope you are ready to do business," he said.

As he spoke, his eyes kept darting around trying to make sure that he knew what was going on at all times. I couldn't blame him because I was doing the exact same thing. I reassured him that I was there to do business.

"I hope you brought the amount we agreed upon," he said, "because I don't do payment plans." Then the motherfucker had the audacity to laugh. I ignored the funny motherfucker.

"I'm a man of my word," I said. So, I opened up the briefcase and let him see the cash, hoping that would put his mind at ease.

"However, I hope the drugs you are giving me are top-notch. I don't want no problems moving them," I said. "If it's high quality, we could become business partners for life."

At that time, the Jamaican Lord summoned about eight men, each holding two duffel bags in each hand. They then handed one over to him. He took one bag of products out of each duffel bag and placed them in front of me at a table. I then summoned Tu Tank over to test out each product.

"I know you like what you see, but I would be careful testing them," he said, "This shit right here might blow your man's mind. He might never recover." Then he started laughing again. That shit was really starting to get irritating. I didn't see what was so fucking funny about a serious business deal such as this.

"This shit ain't no high-quality product," Tu Tank spoke up. "This shit smells and tastes bad like ass. It will never sell on the streets, and we might get a bad reputation for trying to push it. Feel me fam."

When he said that shit, I went from zero to a hundred real quick. My time is just as valuable as my money, and I don't have time to be wasting on no bad dope.

"CHA A FUCKIN LIE!" screamed the Jamaican Lord. "This is the top-of-the-line good shit. You bring your fucking goons in here to insult my product Mon. This fucking retarded ass nigga doesn't know what the fuck he is talking about. Run me my money or else Bumba clot!"

I looked at that nigga. "Go fuck yourself. I'm the wrong nigga to be fucking with."

"Nigga, you don't want to go to war with the Jamaican Mafia Mon. You are outnumbered son," he said.

This nigga just doesn't know who he was fucking with. This nigga had the balls of steel to threaten me and my organization. I don't know how they do in Jamaica, but I was damn sho finna give him a lesson in American culture.

"Go to hell I've never been scared of no nigga." I was getting really pissed. "And I don't take threats lightly."

"Meet you there blood clot," he said. That's when all hell broke loose.

The next thing I knew bullets were flying from every direction and one bullet struck Gino in the shoulder blades. My nigga was screaming at the top of his lungs. That just made me angrier, so two of the Jamaican soldiers got one straight to the dome. D- Black, Tu Tank, and Black Mexican start shooting everyone they saw. I'm so glad I skilled them in marksmanship and defense, cause if I didn't, these niggas would be dead.

Ki and Peanut came running in, blasting when they heard all the commotion. I guess they already killed the few that were outside. Peanut had been shot in the leg and was angry from the pain. That nigga was on a straight adrenaline rush, shooting everything in sight.

The Jamaican Drug Lord with the long dreads pulled out a platinum dessert eagle and shot me dead in the chest. All I could feel was hot lead burning. It seemed as if death had finally come for me. I started coughing and spitting up blood and when my crew saw that I was hit, every Jamaican left in the room dropped like flies. That's how me and my crew roll. If one of us goes down, the other team will lose each and every one of their peers.

They had captured the Jamaican Lord, by shooting that nigga in both his kneecaps. I instructed my crew not to kill him. If it was time to go to hell, he would meet me there. That put a smile on my face. This nigga knew his future and now he was about to be the leading star in his own vision. Damn, I could hardly breathe at this point but before my body went into full shock, that nigga was going to feel my wrath from trying to fuck over my organization. I had the crew pick me up under the arms and walk me over to where that stupid motherfucker lay.

"Please don't kill me Mon, just take the drugs and go. Take it all Mon, just spare my life," he pleaded.

"Nigga everything was so funny earlier, bitch ass nigga why you ain't laughing now," I asked.

Then that nigga dropped a bombshell on me. "Mon, I was sent to kill you, that's it, that's all," he said.

I looked at that nigga like he had three heads. "Continue," I said.

"Some blood clot gave me twenty-five million to make sure you took your last breath before the day is over," he said.

"If it's true, drop the dime," I said.

"Will you spare my life if I tell you?" He asked. I agreed and asked for a name for a second time.

"I truly don't know Mon," he said, "I was told to come to Fort Worth and meet up with you and make sure you took your last breath today. I was supposed to kill you and take the money. That was half of my payment upfront. The drugs were just a decoy to get you here. I never met the main man of the operation."

I looked at the dumbass and said, "Let me formally introduce myself, I'm King Dreadz and now that you have met your maker, it is time for you to go." Then I pumped five hot lead shots into that motherfucker's chest. After that, I got lightheaded and fell to my knees.

"Are you ok?" asked D-Black.

"Nothing a good doctor can't fix," I responded. No one knew how much this shit really hurt. I looked around and noticed Peanut was hit also.

That's when I knew it was time to go. D-black saw the condition I was in, so he started barking orders. That's why that nigga is my right-hand man.

"Everybody listen up, grab all the product, shake down each and every dead motherfucker in here, and get the cashback to the van," D-Black instructed. "In a minute this place is going to be swarming with cops, so we got to get the fuck outta here. Black Mexican go get the gasoline cans. It is time to build a fire. I don't even want these motherfuckers grill to be identified. Gino, Sergio, Danny, and Black Mexican I want yall to shake down these motherfuckers and clean up the crime scene to make sure we don't leave a trace behind."

"On it," Sergio said.

After we finished with everything, we were on our way to the crib but first, we needed to switch cars and torch the vans. It would be uncivilized to be caught slipping because India wouldn't understand one bit so I'm a keep this a little secret. What she doesn't know won't hurt her...

Chapter 4

A Night of Regret

It was a quarter to six in the evening when I made it to Tyrone's house. You know women can never be on time for shit because it takes us forever to get prepared. I had to go down Sunset Boulevard just to beat the traffic. They have been working on that damn freeway forever.

"I hope that I'm not making a big mistake coming over here," I said to myself, as I pulled up at Tyrone's house.

It had been years since I talked to this nigga, since that last time I caught his bitch ass fucking the shit out of my cousin at my own house, in the bed where I lay my head at. Just thinking about it made me sick to my stomach. I hated going down memory lane because it always made me feel some type of way.

I finally got the courage to get out of my car. I walked to the front door and rang the doorbell. I could hear Tyrone's footsteps coming towards the door.

"Who it is?" asked Tyrone.

"It's me India!" I said. "Hurry up and open the door, it's too chilly to be standing out here." *He's such an asshole,* I thought to myself.

The cool breeze made my nipples hard against my dress. Tyrone's funky ass finally open the door to let me in. He was standing at the door, half naked with nothing on but some boxers. I could tell Tyrone was sizing me down because he was smiling too hard.

Once inside, I looked around for a minute. He had flowers in vases and expensive paintings all over the wall. Now I'm over here wondering if this nigga had a little sugar in him. Men hated their manhood being questioned, but hell it was always too funny to watch their facial expressions.

"I like what you have done to the place, Tyrone," I said lying out of my mind.

"Thank you, sweetie, but this really isn't anything spectacular," he quipped.

"Are you sure you don't have a bitch staying here with you," I asked sarcastically. "I'm not trying to get caught up in your shenanigans."

"I am very sure that nobody else stays here with me." Tyrone laughed out loud, "But it would be nice if you would move in with me so that you could keep me company."

Hahaha, this nigga is funny as hell.

"Tell me all about your day, Love," Tyrone said with concern.

"Well for starters," I said, flicking my fingers, "my boss said if I'm late one more time he is going to fire my ass. I can't believe he had the audacity to threaten me."

"Why don't you just quit and find yourself something else to do?" asked Tyrone.

"No, I can't do that. I love working with my bff Irene," I said, my eyes still looking around. I was using the time to make up my mind if I wanted to leave or go ahead.

"Oh, ok I see, so how is ole Irene doing anyway, I bet she still hates my guts huh?"

"Yeah, she really does! She told me I shouldn't have anything else to do with your ass because she doesn't believe one second that you are a changed man, but I'm a grown-ass woman. I can think for myself.

"So, what did you want to talk to me in person about that was so important that you had to talk to me in person?" asked Tyrone.

"I wanted to tell you how bad you hurt me mentally," I said with tears running down my face. "I have been holding these feelings in for a very long time. Why did you have to fuck my cousin and get her pregnant? What did I do to you Tyrone, to be treated this way? I loved you."

Tyrone got up to come put his arms around me. "I'm sorry, I made a very big mistake and karma is kicking my ass."

I started hitting him. "I thought you said you would love me until the end of time. But you went out and pulled some bullshit like this. Why Tyrone, wasn't I good enough for you?" My tears fell like a waterfall, down my face. I couldn't help but relive all the pain I thought I had gone past.

"It just happened," said Tyrone.

He had some damn nerves telling me some bullshit like that.

"How the hell could it just happen?" I asked, ready to slap the shit out of him for saying some bitch ass shit like that. *I swear this nigga is testing me.*

"You were always either working late hours or at them damn clubs with Irene," Tyrone said. "I got so depressed that you weren't spending any time with me, so I confided in your cousin. We started sipping on some wine and started talking about how fucked up our relationship was. The next thing I knew, we were drunk in bed making love. I swear this only happened because I thought you were cheating on me with some other man."

I looked at him in disgust. "So now your dog ass is trying to put all the blame on me. Fuck you hoe ass nigga. I fucking hate you."

Tyrone looked me deep in my eyes and started kissing me. I didn't even try to stop him either. This was so wrong in so many ways, but it felt so good, damn, how I wanted to fuck the shit out of him right now. I could feel the rise of my nipples again yearning for that moment to breathe, so I reached my hands into his boxers and started stroking him until it got rock hard.

Salute soldier, I thought to myself.

Suddenly, I stopped kissing him so I could admire his body, rubbing every inch of his Gladiator Style frame, damn this man is finer than wine. Well, here I was over here, lusting over a man that done me more wrong than good. I took off his boxers and just started kissing and sucking on his manhood. All this chocolate got me craving more, so I put the tip in my mouth nice and slowly. From the look on his face, I could tell that he was enjoying every moment of this. That's when he shoved his big cock in my mouth, forcing me to take that dick. I was breathing heavily, taking it all in, shit I could barely breathe, but I was still handling it like a pro.

"Suck this dick," Tyrone said. "Suck it."

"Hmm yes Daddy, give it to me," I replied.

We fucked around in the living room for a while but somehow, we ended up in his bedroom, that's when it really got intense. I kissed Tyrone all the way to the bed that's when I pushed him down and got on top, riding him like a cowgirl on top of a horse. I came about two times, that shit felt so good I couldn't believe I had that much energy saved in me.

"Turnover," Tyrone moaned out loud. "I want to hit

that pussy from the back."

Being in Doggy style was one of my favorite positions because it's more intense than any other position I know. I could feel it deep inside me. We were both deep in the motion when he started slapping my ass really hard. Fuck yes, I love that hardcore shit—the way he is taking control of this pussy by showing me that he is the King of this jungle.

"Yes, take this pussy, Tarzan!" I yelled out. "This is your pussy. Show me this is your pussy."

Tyrone was fucking the shit out of me, and it felt so good.

"Yes, yes, yes right there, I'm about to cum," I screamed.

I was deep into it and then I heard someone scream, *oh hell no*. I jumped up so fast, not knowing what was happening or what was about to happen. I looked up; I'd be damned. I must be dreaming, please tell me that I'm dreaming. There she was, my own damn cousin and their son, just standing there, staring at us. I couldn't believe I fell for all his lies again. This nigga doesn't give a fuck about me.

Tyrone's face was pale as fuck. It was just like he had just seen a ghost or something. Next thing I knew, my bitch ass cousin came charging at me full speed, trying her hardest to hit me in my face. What the fuck? Did this bitch just hit me in the face? I felt that hit.

"Hell Naw bitch," I yelled, clawing at Jameka's face. I

was so mad that I hit her ass in the face, with a three-piece special and connected with a side order. Damn, that felt so good, getting back at her for fucking up my relationship.

Smack! The thud landed on my face.

"Wtf?" I looked up and saw that Tyrone had slapped the shit out of me. I could tell that he was really pissed off from the look on his face.

"STUPID BITCH YOU DONE HURT HER WITH YOUR CRAZY ASS," Tyrone Screamed.

Ok motherfucka ya bitch ass is going to pay for this watch and see nigga, I thought to myself.

"Get the fuck out my house crazy ass bitch before I throw you out," screamed Tyrone.

I put all my clothes back on as I ran out of the house, crying to my car. As I was driving, I started thinking about what the hell just happened. I knew I shouldn't have gotten back in contact with him, every time Irene told me something that I shouldn't do I never took her advice. I don't even know how Kent'e was going to take this if he found out Tyrone slapped me in my face. *I must keep this a secret from him.*

I tried calling Irene but didn't get an answer. "Please pick up, please pick up I don't know what the fuck to do about this situation." After the fourth time of calling, she finally picked up.

"Hello," Irene said, in a really tired voice.

"I'm so sorry to wake you up." I started sobbing up a

storm. "But I really need to talk to you."

"What's wrong, India," asked Irene, "I knew it had to be an emergency for you to call so late."

I began telling her about the hot mess I had gotten myself into.

"Can I spend the night?" I asked.

"Yes, girl you know you are always welcome to come over here anytime you like," said Irene. "I told you from day one not to fuck with that nigga. Why do you always pick these goofy ass niggas over the good ones."

"I don't know."

"You still haven't learned your damn lesson girl. Why are you trying to make King suffer for all your stupid mistakes?"

I started crying when she told me that.

"Girl, you know I love you, but I just don't want to see you getting hurt anymore that's all. You know you are going to have to tell King one of these days or it's going to eat you up inside."

"I know I know." I was still crying my eyes out. "I didn't mean to fuck around on him like that. It was just in the heat of the moment."

Irene kept on bitching at me until she told me that she would talk more to me when I made it to her house.

"Ok." I hung up the call.

As soon as I got off the phone, I started thinking about how I was going to tell King about this. He was not going to like the fact that I was over there. Damn, I had gotten myself into a rut. It was very stupid of me to go over to Tyrone's house. I don't know why I didn't listen to Irene.

I finally made it to Irene's two-story brick house in Crowley. It had maroon bricks with gold trimmings and a big ass front yard.

I love this neighborhood; I wonder how much her rent is. I sure hope she remembered to keep the door unlocked as she told me.

I walk to the door and turn the knob. There she was, sitting on the couch and dressed in a black nightgown, with a box of tissue and a cold icepack.

"Hey girlie," I said, "I'm so glad that you let me come over."

"It's no problem. You know you are always welcome to come whenever you feel like it, said Irene. We are family."

I gave her the biggest hug I could ever give a person. She handed me the ice pack so I could put it on my eye.

"Damn, my eye hurts badly," I mumble to myself.

"What happened, India?" Irene asked, staring at me like I was a little lost soul.

"Girl, it's a long story," I replied, putting my head in my hands so Irene couldn't look me in the eyes.

"No rush," Irene quipped. "We have all the time in the world. Are you hungry? Would you like anything to drink? I have water, tea, diet coke, or some orange juice."

"Yes, I'm hungry. I haven't eaten anything since our

lunch break earlier.

"Ok bestie, make yourself at home," Irene replied, making her way to the kitchen.

"And I would like a glass of sweet tea please," I called out after her.

I love Irene so much and she has been by my side, through all my ups and downs. Not once has she ever sugar-coated anything to me. What would I have done if I didn't have her in my corner?

There I was sitting there, all lost in thoughts when Irene came out of the kitchen with a turkey sandwich with all the works—pickles on the side, a bag of baked potato chips, and a tall glass of sweet tea.

"Oh my, this is a feast, Irene," I said.

"Girl, you need to relax, everything will be okay just watch and see," Irene quipped, as she started giving me a massage.

"I sure hope you are right," I replied, taking a bite of the turkey sandwich. "Hmmm this sandwich is so good and don't let me get started on this massage."

After I finished eating my delicious sandwich, we talked for about an hour.

"Well India, it was nice talking to you but I'm about to go to sleep and you already know where the guest room is."

"OK, thanks for everything, Irene. Good night, I love you."

"Good night, India and I love you too." Irene headed to

her room.

I needed a long hot bubble bath so that I could think about how fucked up my life was at that moment. After I finished my nice relaxing bath, I got out so I could dry off. Afterward, I quickly dressed up in the red and black checkered nightgown Irene had provided.

As I lay in the bed, slowly I drifted off into deep sleep, promising myself that tomorrow would be a better day.

Chapter 5

A Nightmarish Turn of Events

The sweet taste of blood always got my soul running. I really didn't want the situation to get out of control like it did, but hey if you fuck with the M.O.B Cryme Family, you're bound to get done in.

I sat in the living room and looked around, wondering if Gramps was in his room because I really needed to talk to him. Gramps was the only person that really understood me. So, I got my lazy ass up and knocked on his bedroom door.

''Knock, knock,'' I said, rapping softly on his door.

"Come on in," said Gramps from inside.

"What's up Gramps how are you? I really need to holla at you for a brief moment."

"I'm doing okay, son—just sitting here watching the news. The police just found twenty dead Jamaicans. They say they would bring down whoever was responsible for this murderous act."

Damn! News sure does travel fast.

"What did you want to talk to me about son?" Gramps turned to me.

"Well Gramps, it's like this." I scratched my head. "I know you already know that I had something to do with this little incident that happened on the news. I don't know how the laws found out about it unless somebody lived to tell the story."

"I see," said Gramps.

"It got out of hand; it was just supposed to be a simple deal but them hoes tried to play us like some clowns. Somebody set us up!" I was becoming angry again.

"Would you like a drink?"

"I don't mind."

Gramps walked over to the bar poured a bottle of Whiskey into two glasses and handed one glass to me. We drank in silence for a while and then I spoke.

"When my parents died, you were the one that raised me up, to do what was right. Your number one rule was, 'If anyone ever tries to step on your toes, strike them before they strike you'."

"I also taught you to keep your enemies close and your friends closer," said Gramps.

"When I got shot in my chest, it felt as if I was about to die." I took a sip of my drink, "But it only made me stronger. I had to go to my personal doctor so he could take out the bullet and fix up my war wound, but strangely, I can still feel the pain."

"Did you clean up the scene before you left?" asked Gramps, as he was pouring himself another glass of Whiskey.

"Yes, we did everything that needed to be done. The police won't find anything to point fingers at us," I replied. He was very impressed with my war tactics when I told him about how much dope we got out of the good deal gone bad.

"Where is your sister and troublesome brother?"

"They are both at Club 2010 XL for tonight, but they shall return early in the morning."

"Ok, if you see Sergio before I do, please tell him to keep his ass out of trouble because Justin can't keep bailing him out of trouble."

"Yes sir, I will deliver your message as soon as I see him. Can I ask you a quick question?"

"Go ahead, son," Gramps said, as he poured a third glass. I really wanted to tell him that he needed to slow down on all that drinking, but that would have been a suicidal move.

"Did you see India at any time today?" I asked.

"Not at all. Did you try calling her?"

"I did, but it went straight to voicemail. I am kinda

worried."

I was even more worried now that Gramps said she did not come around. It wasn't like her to not call or come around to check on me.

After I finished talking about everything I needed to talk about, I went into my room to do some more studying on 48 Laws of Power, a book written by Robert Greene.

It was 11 o'clock pm when India decided to come home. *I'm really going to give her a piece of my mind because how in the fuck does she think she can just come home anytime she felt like it?*

I lost my anger and instead became worried the moment my eyes fell on her. I was startled by the bruises on her face.

I jumped up quickly and rushed to her. "Baby, are you ok? Who did this to you?"

India started crying and screaming. "There is this man named Willie Joe. He raped me and beat me up. He said he would kill me if I went to the police."

I clenched my fist as anger took all over me. *That nigga done fucked up big time, so now he is going to have to pay the consequences for his mischievous behavior.*

I had zero tolerance when it came to my woman and family, so I was definitely going to get to the bottom of this.

"Where have you been I have been trying to call you?" I asked India.

"I spent the night at Irene. I didn't want you to be too

worried about me, but I'm truly sorry babe. I should have come to you first in my time of need," she replied, cleaning snot from her face.

I heard everything she said, but to me, she sounded more like the teacher from the Charlie Brown cartoon.

"Baby, baby," India said, "Were you even paying attention to anything I have been telling you?"

I'm not even going to lie, I was not paying attention, but I lied anyway. "Yes, I heard everything you told me."

"Can we please go get something to eat?" India said, as rubbed her belly.

"Okay, baby. Meet me in the den in a couple of minutes. I need to make a couple of calls," I told her.

I called my sister Ki to give her the rundown on India's situation. I could hear in the tone of her voice that she was very pissed and that she would keep her eyes and ears on what was going on in the streets. The last call I made was to my associate Ted Dawson. I made a reservation for two at his 5-star restaurant. He had the only Italian restaurant that stayed open during the wee hours. If it weren't for me, that place wouldn't be shit. Wherever I go, the crowd follows me like a trend, but one thing I know for sure, I can always depend on his services.

When my baby came downstairs, I almost jumped off the couch because she was looking sexy as fuck, with her hair fixed, makeup on her face, and a nicely fitted black Prada dress that showed the curves of her frame.

"Hmm mm, hello nurse," I said. I loved it when she had her toes done and don't let me get started on the perfume that she was wearing. I was so lusting after her, but who wouldn't want a badass chick like mine?

I was dressed in a black tailored, slim-fitted suit with the iced-out cufflinks and black loafers; I had to throw on my Dobb hat that matched my suit. I knew one damn thing for sure we are always going to look our best wherever we go. My baby and I look like Michelle and Barack Obama, so I knew we were going to turn some heads when we stepped through the door.

The restaurant was packed as fuck, but my associate Ted made sure that we bypassed everyone that was in line waiting. I could feel the tension of the crowd staring at us, trying to figure out who we were and why were we getting this A1 VIP treatment.

When we finally made it to our table, it was set up beautifully with peach-scented candles and red fresh roses. I pulled my baby seat out so she could have a seat, but I got all sidetracked when this yellow bone with a big ass and tits, come over to our table with some menus in her hand, so we can order our food.

It all started with a smile from me that made the waitress blush, but I could feel the heat of India's temper rising from the whole incident. She always got jealous when other women flirted with me but I always reassured her every time that me and her are bound forever.

When I saw her facial expression of disgust, I started laughing. "I know you are not getting all jealous."

"Whatever, nigga." She rolled her eyes. "Keep on playing with me, I'm a drop that hoe."

"Why are you so violent? She didn't do anything to you?" She looked up at me like, *you really want me to answer that question*? I wondered how the waitress was feeling at this moment because she hadn't said a word this whole entire time.

We picked up the menus to look at them for a brief moment, damn everything looks so delicious.

I looked at the waitress and placed my order. "I'll have the veal and asparagus in cream white wine sauce, smoky chasse with mushrooms over bowtie pasta, some cheese bread, Caesar salad, and a bottle of your finest red wine."

India ordered the same thing, but the only difference was she wanted a glass of pomegranate Cosmo. I wondered what the hell that was.

"Baby," I started, "When we get done with our meal, is there any other place you would like to go, because this is your night, so enjoy the mood."

"Yes," India said. "I've been dying to go to the Hyena comedy club that's in downtown Dallas."

"Ok, baby, your wish is my command," I replied. "I love it when my future wife is happy."

When our food finally arrived at our table, damn was all I could say, because everything smelled so good. I took one bite into the veal and it just melted in my mouth. One thing that I don't do is bullshit when it comes to my food. Once done with our meal and drinks, I called the sexy waitress over to order a molten chocolate cake so I could feed my baby. She was the only person in the world that meant a lot to me, besides my family.

I got up and wiped my mouth with a napkin and gave India a nice passionate kiss. "Baby, I will be right back. I'm about to talk to Ted about some business in his office, so you can order yourself another round to drink."

I opened the door to Ted's office and there he was, sitting at his desk, doing some paperwork.

I was very impressed with how clean it was in there, besides the ball-up paper on the floor.

"Hey, my man! I would like to start off by thanking you for this beautiful night. Everything was so perfect." I shook hands with him.

"What's been going on with you, old friend?" I asked as I took a seat on his couch. Ted was looking nervous as hell and I could tell something was bothering him.

"I've been trying to get in contact with you King. I need a small favor, but I will pay you back with interest."

"What kind of favor?"

"I would like to put out a contract on these two motherfuckers," Ted said, showing me the photos. "They have been trying to extort me for money saying that they will burn down the building if I don't start paying up."

"I will take care of it, so don't worry about a thing," I replied, while I kept examining the pictures. *Damn, these two cats look really familiar. Oh, snap that's David Rico and Charlie Brown.* I got very upset and worried about this situation.

"What am I going to get in return for my services old friend?" I asked.

"I would give you another 10% of the restaurant income plus $20,000 upfront. I already know that you are a successful businessman, and my money is chump change to you, however, I really do need your help."

I began thinking, wondering how I wanted to handle this situation, knowing damn well I really didn't want to bring any drama to my organization because I know this mission could get crucial if not planned right.

"Don't worry Ted, I got you." I made a private call to my source, Officer Williams, to get a rundown on David Rico and Charlie Brown. After I got off the phone with him, I called D-Black and gave him the plan on how I wanted the plan to go.

I *hope and pray that everything goes as planned.*

Damn, I am so tired.

I finally made it back to the table where India was sitting.

"I'm ready babe, let's go." I took out two hundred dollars so I could tip the waitress for her outstanding services. By the time we made it out the door, the waitress was right behind us. She caught up to us and gave me one of the wettest kisses ever. Then she gave me a card and whispered in my ear, 'My name's Angie. You can call me anytime.

"No, you didn't just disrespect me in front of my face like that," India said, as she lunged at the waitress and tightened her hands around her neck in a chokehold. "You are going to learn today BITCH about keeping your hands off what's mines."

Damn! I had to get her up off that girl because she could barely breathe, and I didn't want her to kill her.

It took me a while to calm India down. I have never seen her this way before. As we were walking towards the car, four huge men jumped out of a parked van, with masks on their faces. One of them grabbed India and held her so she couldn't get away. She screamed for me to come to help her. I tried to run to her aid, but someone hit me upside my head and knocked me out unconscious.

When I finally woke up, I was tied up in a smelly dark room. I could tell that I was fucked up badly from that blow to the head by how swollen my face was. Damn, I couldn't see shit. As I looked up again, there stood the four masked men from the parking lot, standing at least five to ten feet in front of me. The same man who grabbed India still had her captive.

"If you hurt her, I promise to God I will kill all of you hoes," I said trying to break myself free to save her.

When I said that, two of the men came my way and started hitting me in my bloody face with their fists, as hard as they could. I screamed in great pain wishing they would just kill me to get it over with.

All I heard was India crying saying, 'Get away from him! Oh, God! Somebody, please help, they are killing him.'

Knowing how my baby was, I knew for a fact that she was over there clawing at that nigga to let her go.

All the shit I had ever done in my life was finally catching up to me. I could not believe that it took this long before somebody decided to finish me off. There was no telling who the four masked men were because I made so many enemies when I first came up in this dope game.

The two men finally decided to stop beating me because it was so quiet you could hear a pin drop. India ran to my aid, so she could comfort me.

"My poor baby," said India, as she wiped my face off with her dress.

"Are you okay baby? Did those bastards do anything to hurt you?" I asked, coughing up blood.

"No, they just held me back, so I couldn't stop them from hurting you. They fucked you up real bad, baby."

"I promise if I live through this, they are going to pay for what they have done."

As I was sitting there I just blacked out, thinking about all the people I had killed over the years. Gramps was right when he told me that there would be days like this, but I never thought it would happen to me.

Man, I wish I would have listened to India when she said

we needed a change. NOW HERE I WAS, A VICTIM OF MY OWN Environment, daydreaming about how my life came to this point............

Chapter 6

The Day My World Changed Forever

I was just a simple sixteen-year-old teenager, who had more problems than I could handle at my age, but I still learned to cope with my issues. I was born in the slums of Stop Six, Texas, where there were a lot of murders, hustling, crackheads, bloods, boppas, and even the roaches were taking over.

I was very close to my mother than I was to my father. My mother was a loving caring person that always did her best to raise her kids up right because for one, she was very overprotective about us.

We were not allowed to play with other kids our age, because the street we lived on was infested with a lot of drugs and killing.

However, with my father, it was a completely different ball game. He was a well-known block hustle, that demanded respect in these streets. He taught us to never fear anyone because they could bleed just as quickly as we could. Everybody seemed to respect his hustle, but the haters couldn't stand his ass. They robbed him, beat him, and shot him, but he kept getting stronger and stronger each time. He always made sure that his family was taken care of by any means necessary.

My little sister Ki was fifteen years old at the time. Everyone knew that she was a daddy's girl so if they touched her in any way, it was an automatic death sentence. My brother and I hated the fact that she always got things from him. One thing about my sister was the fact that she always made straight A's in school.

Then there was my younger brother Sergio, who was fourteen years old. My poor mother had her hands full with that child right there. She used to tell him that he was so much like our father when he was younger. Sergio got kicked out of school so much at an early age that our mother got tired of it and enrolled him in home school. He got his act together after doing a year in his mother's class. Lol, he was begging to go back to regular school.

My Gramps was a wise old man who always told us a lot of urban stories and gave us the wisdom to abide by them. My uncle Mike—I really didn't know too much about him besides hearing Urban Legend Tales in the Hood saying that he and my grandfather were tied in the Macedonia Mafia in the early 70s. Mr. Macedonia was a well-known drug lord in the hood and everything had to go through him first before it could even get out on the streets.

Everything was going smoothly in my life until the summertime when I was awakened by a phone call, early Saturday morning. It was the news of my parent's death.

When the Detective told me that, it felt like someone just took part of my life away. I sure hated to be the bearer of bad news to my siblings, but I still had to tell them.

After I hung up the phone with the Detective, I couldn't do anything but drop my head down and tears started to flow like an ocean.

At that time Ki was walking by, on her way to the kitchen, but stopped in her tracks just to see what was wrong with me.

"I have some bad news, which I have to share with you and Sergio," I said.

Ki hurried up to get our little brother so they could see what the hell was going on. All I heard were footsteps echoing on the floor as they ran back to where I was sitting. I was still terrified by the news I had just received.

"What's up bro, what the hell is going on?" asked Sergio.

"The police just found Mom and Dad dead behind an alleyway, burned to death. They said they couldn't identify the bodies because they were fucked off."

"No Kent'e," said Ki, "Don't say no shit like that. They will return back in a few, just watch and see."

Sergio was so mad that he stormed out of the house, knocking over shit. I felt so sorry for my brother and sister. In my heart I wished I could tell them that this was all a dream and that our parents would be back home, but hey who was I fooling? Reality is a bitch that we all must face. *I sure hope that boy does not get himself caught up in any trouble, but I can't run after him right now I have to tend to Ki.*

"It will be okay," I said to Ki, rubbing her back as she sobbed, knowing damn well they were never coming back. We would never see the light of them again unless we died and went to Heaven. At that very moment, my life began to change for the worse.

"Why? Why did someone have to take them away from us," Ki said, crying her eyes out, "And what did they do to deserve this type of horrific treatment?"

I was hurting so deep inside that it was fucking me up mentally, knowing damn well that this wasn't some dream.

"Ki, we are all that we have now, so we have to be strong for each other," I said. I sat there and comforted her on the couch until she fell asleep, all the while wondering where the hell Sergio was.

Sergio came back to the house about three hours later. I could tell he was a little mellowed because I didn't hear him knocking shit over or punching the wall, but when I looked at his face, I could tell that there was something odd and strange about it.

"What the hell did you do this time?" I asked Sergio, noticing that he had blood on his clothes.

"Nigga, I'm a grown ass man and I don't have to answer to anyone because you ain't my daddy and you sure hell ain't my momma, so fuck off," Sergio said, with a crooked grin on his face.

Man, oh man, I could already tell that I would have my hands full dealing with his ass. Without thinking, I reached back and slapped the shit out of his ass. My mind was so cloudy that I couldn't think. Today was not one of those days and I clearly did not want to get into any issues with Sergio, but the deed was done now.

"NIGGA FUCK YOU," he said with rage and punched me dead in the eye.

Ouch! He hit me so hard that I started seeing stars. I was so furious my blood began to boil. I activated my Hulk mode and was ready to smash. I jumped up so fast without thinking and caught him with a right hook to the jaw. Now we were both mad as hell and all you could hear was shit falling on the ground from all that tussling we were doing.

Ki woke up screaming from the top of her lungs telling us that we need to stop trying to kill each other. Damn, the shit she was telling us was right. Here we were acting like some damn savages when we just got some fucked up news about our parents.

I had to respect my sister's wishes because she was already facing a tragic event and she didn't need any more stress added to the equation. So, I had to be a man. I stood up and gave Sergio my hand so that I could help him up off the ground.

"No hard feelings," I told my bro.

"Same here," he replied.

That made Ki so happy that she came and hugged the both of us, with a nice bear hug.

"Now this is what I call a family, just the three of us, the muthafuckan Three Amigos. We don't need to be fighting each other," I said. "I'm so sorry I took out all my anger on you bro."

"It's not your fault. I was the one who was talking shit first, so I got what I deserved," said Sergio.

"I'm really going to miss them a lot," Ki said like it was their fault somehow, but I had to reassure her that it wasn't any of our fault and whoever did this was going to have to accept their fate someday soon.

After we finished talking, we said our prayers so we could get a good night's rest. As I lay in my bed, I began to cry to myself, mumbling the words "I am my mother and father's keeper, and the ones that killed them are going to pay the price."

When I stopped feeling sorry for myself, I got down on my knees to say a prayer for my parents' souls to rest in peace. Lord knows maybe I was having a nightmare that night and haven't woken up just yet.

Chapter 7

Schoolyard Drama

It was two weeks since the funeral; everyone was affected mentally because of the tragedy of my parent's death, especially me. I couldn't believe how many people showed up that day! I was very impressed; if I counted right there were at least a thousand or more people.

But the one person I didn't expect to meet was the Urban Legend himself, Mr. Macedonia. There he was, live in living color, he had so much swag to him that it made those hustlers look like trash.

"I'm so sorry about your parents," Mr. Macedonia said to me. "I wonder why it had to come down to this because they were some very good people. He kept going on about how much he loved and respected my parents, so he gave me his card, telling me that if I ever wanted a job, I could come to work for him. Just that thought alone made me happy, that a man as big as he would want someone like me working for him.

After the funeral, everyone showed their respect to one another and then went their separate ways.

My brother, sister, and I had to move in with Gramps because no one else wanted to take us in, but at that time Uncle Mike was in jail for supposedly killing a cop so we were very grateful that our grandfather took us in.

That night, Gramps told us so many stories about our parents that we never knew before, going into every little detail saying that everyone portrayed them as the great Bonnie & Clyde duel that had each other's back no matter what type of situation they were in.

His stories were very fascinating to the point that I was ready for more.

This really was the first time that my siblings and I had ever been to Gramps' house before. I just could not imagine how much money he had to stay in a nice house like this. I never really have been in a two-story house with six bedrooms, four baths, a game room, and an in-house theater that was whipped to the fullest. He even had a pool house with a pool that was much bigger than any pool I had ever swum in before. My siblings and I were equipped with our own bedrooms which had our very own TVs.

A very odd thought popped up in my mind, I wonder

why he was never in our lives up until my parents died. Just the thought of that bothered me a lot, but I thought that maybe I was just over here tripping about nothing.

Ring.... Ring... Riiinnnngggggggg goes the alarm.

I swung at the alarm clock and missed, but when it came to the second swing, it flew off my nightstand. Damn, I couldn't believe how tired I was. I needed more sleep, damn it; I yawned. The first day of school always got to me but thank the Lord that we still got to go to our old school in Stop Six.

"Y'all need to hurry up," I said impatiently. "I'm not trying to be late for the first day of school."

Like, it really mattered what time we got there. I couldn't figure out why I was so anxious to get there.

It seemed as if Ki didn't care too much about school anymore since the death of our parents, but I could understand why my brother was taking his sweet little time. He never did like school. He always told me that. The slowpoke was finally ready, and we were on our way to school. When we made it to school, we had to go in three different directions. Thanks to Sergio, we had missed breakfast, and I was starving. I could tell by the way my stomach was growling.

It was now lunchtime I literally ran to the cafeteria so I could eat some grub, but what took me by surprise was when I saw this very big crowd of people that was crowded around this one particular table, and everyone was bobbing their heads. I went over to the table to see what the big commotion was all about, One dude was beating on the table and this other dude was just riding with the beat. Damn, that was some of the nicest shit I have ever heard before. I had to get a little closer so I could hear more. I was bobbing my head, getting into the groove until this one nigga said, "Who called this bitch ass nigga over to our table?" Everyone stopped and stared at me like I had shit all over me.

At that very moment, I got all up in his face and said, "So who are you calling a bitch nigga," not giving a fuck if my odds were twenty-five to one. It ain't no punk in my blood.

"This nigga got some balls," he said cracking his knuckles like he was ready to throw down. "He must don't know who I am."

I pumped up my nuts even more and said "Nigga, I really don't give a fuck who you are, to me you are a bitch ass nigga," and I popped him right in the mouth. I hit that nigga so hard he slid out of that chair.

Everyone that was around us was stunned that I did him like that; even this one fine chick came to see what was really going on.

"That's enough, little nigga," some big dude said, laughing hard as a motherfucker. I did what he said and got off that nigga because I'm not looking for no more trouble, damn this school year is already turning out bad.

"Say Dee, you got your ass kicked, nigga," the big dude said still laughing. "Didn't I tell you that if you keep on talking all that shit, one day somebody was going to kick your ass? Now look at you."

When he said that everyone started laughing and giving me daps like I was their savior or something, but what I didn't know was that I had just beat up the school bully. Damn, that was all I needed to hear. Now I had to watch my back wherever I went.

"My name is T-Money," the big dude said, as he gave me some dap, "What's your name, little homie?"

"Everyone calls me Kent'e, but I go by the name KJ for short."

"Oh really, like Kunta Kinte," he said jokingly.

I started laughing. *I'm dealing with all kinds of clowns today,* I thought to myself, but T-Money seemed cool as fuck, but for some reason, I didn't see him as a threat to me.

"Say Dough-Dough kick a beat," my new friend said, "Say homie do you know how to rap or something?"

"I got a little something, something."

"Well gone spit something and give us G's a taste of that anger, bro."

Now that I had gone and put my foot in my mouth, I had to think of something real quick and hurry because everyone was in my grill. I just started freestyling...

{ I never gave a fuck about no lame ass nigga, keep

running off the mouth we gonna see who much bigga, I pulled the trigga, and watch him fade out like a genie, just like Houdini, so nigga want you to come and see me, you want to be me, but you're a bitch in my eyes, I took you as a fuck nigga, but it ain't no surprise, young dumb and stupid but you're ready to die, talking about your a gangsta, but we know that's a lie, Ha, Ha, don't cry, just take it as a lesson, before these bullets come pouring down on you like a blessing, I play no game boy, this ain't no game of Tetris, young fly and dangerous with blood stains on my necklace}....

I had everyone in the cafeteria going all the way live, screaming "that nigga got some mad skills."

There was so much noise in there that the school security and police had to see what the big commotion was all about. I could hear whispers in the air with some of the ladies saying "Girl he is a cutie; I wonder if he has a girlfriend," and one even said, "He can get this pooh nanny anytime he likes."

I could feel the tension in the air that someone was plotting to do something to me, and boy was I right, there he was, the devil himself staring right at me.

I was glad when lunchtime was finally over. I was trying to hurry up to class when T-Money said, "Wait up lil homie. I just wanted you to know that I fuck with you, so you can hang with me anytime." From that moment on, me and him became blood brothers from another momma.

As I was sitting there minding my own damn business, that nigga Dee came over to my desk and whispered the words, "Don't let me catch you after school, because you already know what time it is."

To me, that felt like a threat, and I take my life seriously.

That day just wasn't my day, because who would ever know the odds of him being in one of my classes, especially six rows behind? All he had to do was sneak up behind me if he really wanted to.

After school, I tried to locate Ki, Sergio, and T-Money to fill them in on everything that was going down. I came across my sister and bro, but someone mentioned to me that Money had left early.

The crowd was getting thick as hell outdoors, everyone must have heard that it was about to go down after school, because people were coming from everywhere and I mean everywhere, rushing to make it to the empty field. I looked around my surroundings, but I didn't see him or his goons around anywhere. The first thing that came to my mind was, maybe he had chickened out or gone to get a gun so he could use it on me. I know the chicken part is out the door because dealing with a nigga like Dee, I know he is not going to stop until he has my head on a platter.

"Where they at?" asked Sergio, pacing back and forward ready for whatever. "Them marks got the game fucked up if they think they are going to jump my brother."

I'm not even going to lie, I was nervous as fuck, not knowing what I was about to face at this moment. All I could hear was a bunch of deep whispering.

I feel sorry for him.

I think Dee went home to get a gun.

Maybe I was tripping or just imagining things for no reason, but what stood out to me the most was Ki's *One for All, All for One statement.* I looked over her way and noticed that she was checking to make sure that her black and pink Nike was laced up to the T. One thing I know for sure my sister might be a girl but deep down inside she had more heart than any man I knew.

It was very hot, and my body began to sweat like I had been running on the football field all day. Now here it was, a quarter past three and the crowd began to get thicker and thicker but that only could mean one thing, that Dee and his boys were on their way.

I looked at Sergio and Ki and gave them a nod just to let them know to be ready. We normally would have some type of backup plan but not at this very moment there wasn't a plan A to be used whatsoever.

"There he is," Dee said. "I really didn't think that he would have the balls to show up. And look how cute the lil faggot brought his little sis and brother to help him fight his battle."

"FUCK YOU," said Ki with her fist balled up ready to strike anyone who made any type of wrong move.

"NAW FUCK YOU AND YOUR WEAK ASS FAMI-
LY," one of his crew said as he tried to slap my sister in the
face but ended up missing.

No, that bastard didn't just try to hit my sister in her
face. I sidestepped that nigga and hit him with a two-piece
special. Dee and his other friend with the Jerry curl ran up
to help their other friend who was getting the shit beat out
of him by Sergio.

I was on Dee's ass like white on rice, all you could hear
was, "Get that nigga, Kent'e, beat his ass. It felt really good
being on the winning side until a few random people came
out of nowhere and started attacking me. I don't know
who it was, but somebody knocked me on my ass, and
as soon as I hit the ground someone started kicking the
shit out of me. Wow! I really wasn't expecting that shit,
motherfuckers nowadays don't even fight fair! As I was
getting my ass beat, I could hear my brother and sister
begging for someone to come help them. I felt really bad
that I couldn't come to their aid.

I got so dizzy I started spitting up blood and hallucinat-
ing that the police were putting handcuffs on me. That day
didn't seem real whatsoever, because when I finally woke
up I realized that it wasn't a dream at all.

Gramps came to pick us up from the Juvenile Detention
Center. I told him everything that went down and how he
disrespected our family. Gramps wasn't mad he was very
proud of us for defending our family honor.

The principal at the school had suspended us for three days since we had never been in trouble before, but once I went back, everyone was on my jock. Worshiping me like I was some kind of hero even the woman was asking me if I had a girlfriend on my team. I told them that I was rocking solo, but I was looking for someone special. But really on the cool, I had my eye on this one chick who went by the name Strawberry, nobody else didn't even matter to me.

After school, I met up with T-Money, he told me that he liked my style so much that he was going to put me under his wings with the dope game hustle. I was so ready to become a man thinking that this was a perfect opportunity to become one.

That nigga T-Money was so fun to be around. He had given me the game freely, free of charge. I started off with a couple of nickel-and-dime bags of weed running through it like I was a real boss.

One bright day, T-Money decided to take me to his house. That's when I met his skinny younger brother, Trayvon D. Black. That nigga was a year younger than Sergio, but there was something I liked about him. He reminded me of myself when I was his age. He was completely different from his big bro.

The block I hustled on was on the East Side of Ramey Street, a small street that was located in Stop Six. There were a whole lot of haters on my turf; it got so bad niggas started jacking me for my money and dope. I got so tired of it that I went to buy a 9 mm, hot off the streets. I was nervous as hell when I first carried it. It was just that the thought of me killing someone creeped me out. I got out of that shell really quick when niggas kept on doing all that fuck shit to me. It didn't take me long to get well-known in the hood whatsoever.

One time this nigga pulled out a 357 on me with no damn bullets in the gun or chamber. At first, I was scared at the fact he had the gun against my temple. That night, I prayed to God that I wouldn't die, but I had to protect myself even if it meant going out like a soldier.

I quickly pulled out my gun and shot him in the leg. When he saw how serious shit was, he tried to run from the situation but I stayed on his ass, not letting him get anywhere. That's when I really realized that he didn't have any bullets.

"Nigga how are you going to rob someone with no bullets?" I asked, aiming my heater at him. "I should take you off this earth right now."

"I'm so sorry," he pleaded.

I was so pissed off that I wanted to shoot him again, but instead, I put up my gun and beat his ass, to teach him a lesson on playing with grown folks.

I've been in so many gun battles and fights with niggas that I'm surprised that I'm still breathing.

That nigga T-Money was so impressed with how I handled my business that he graduated me from weed to moving crack. Crack was a totally different ball game from weed.

I was raking in so much money with this hustle that I bought myself a Pinto at a Motor Used car lot. I know it wasn't much to look at, but hey at least it was something for me to get around in.

I felt a little envy when I saw that the other dealers were rolling Cadillac, Caprice classics, beamers, and Lexus, but T-Money reassured me that it was not wise to bring heat upon myself. Boy, was he right? One of the flashy dealers always ends up getting busted or killed.

When I moved up in rank, I started making more percentage of money. T-Money always made sure I was taken care of no matter what. I had enough money that I could buy myself a Cadillac Seville if I really wanted to, but I decided to save my money for a better cause.

I don't know if Gramps knew what I was doing but I had to tell him what was going on with me. So, one day, I 'fessed up.

"Gramps, I want you to know that I am making money hustling drugs," I said to him.

"I already knew, just by looking at all your fancy jewelry, expensive clothes, shoes, and all the small stuff that you buy for your siblings," Gramps said and started to rub his temple. "I really need you to be really careful of your surroundings. Don't put too much trust in friends and respect the game."

"Gramps, I know I don't have to be doing this. I just want to be my own man by making my own money, without depending on anyone."

"Son you are so much like your father that it scares me. That's why I'm humble myself by teaching you everything I taught him at your age. I want to tell you something that I have been keeping from you. Your Father was a part of the Macedonia Mafia but got out of it before you were born."

What Gramps didn't know was that I already knew this information from a couple of old cats from the hood, but I still acted surprised when he told me.

"And your mother is Tony Macedonia's daughter," he said.

Oh, really? I must have heard that wrong. Tony is my mother's daddy. The sound of that played over and over in my head. Now that's one piece of information that was kept from me, from my informants. I wonder if they knew that or not. I had so many thoughts running through my head. Unanswered questions needed to be asked.

"Tony never did like the fact that your father and mother were together. He tried to break them up so many times by sending random women to see him, sending him on crash dummy missions, and a couple of other things. He left them alone when he realized that their love was truly unbreakable but what really put the icing on the cake was when you came along."

"How come they never told me this?" I asked, wanting to know the truth. I felt so betrayed.

"They wanted to keep you away from him and his ways. Tony is the full devil in disguise. There's so much you don't know about him."

I can't believe that my own parents will keep my grandfather away from me, not one, but both of them.

Gramps kept going on and on about something, but I really wasn't paying attention. I decided I wouldn't tell Ki or Sergio what I just found out because that would truly devastate them, so I kept this secret to myself. From that moment alone, I knew where I wanted to go with my life.

Chapter 8

Unraveling Vengeance: Secrets and Retribution

F our years after my parents died, we still put flowers on their graves every now and then. Once my hustle game got supreme and icy, I decided to move out of my Gramps' house and rent my own apartment.

Time changed and people changed a lot, except my brother. He had been arrested twice for assault, so I had moved him in with me. I took on the responsibility to keep him out of trouble, so I gave him a couple of side missions to prove himself worldly. My sister Ki moved back with Gramps to get a break from college for a while. I was very proud of her for graduating from high school. Despite being two years late, I still ended up throwing her one of the biggest parties ever. We had so much fun that night.

In my spare time when I wasn't hustling, I was taking night classes to get my GED. Things were starting to get better for me and my family, we put the past behind us so we could worry about the future.

That nigga Dee kept going to jail for dumb shit, so he wasn't really worried about me no more. But every time we came across one another, we would look each other up and down but went on with our business. To this day, I have flashbacks from that one incident in high school but boy how I wanted to murk that nigga.

One day I was riding with my boy T-Money, Sergio, and Trayvon, which I ended up giving him the name D-Black. We were on our way to the club to see U.G.K perform when this van pulled up right beside us with guns hanging out the window.

I felt it way deep down in my soul that some shit was about to go down. All I saw were three dudes dressed in black with ski masks on their faces, they all had some type of high-power gun pointed right at us. One of them was so demanding for us to give up our jewelry, shoes, money, and other valuable materials. I wanted to pull out my hammer so badly, but I didn't want to make the wrong move on getting us killed. The nigga that was talking, sounded really familiar like I knew him from somewhere.

"Fuck you hoe ass nigga," said T-Money, "we ain't giving you a bitch ass shit."

When he said that, them niggas just began letting loose inside the car. D-Black and Sergio were ducked down in the back seat.

"They killed my brother," D-Black said, crying a river. As I got out, I started running towards the van when someone shot me in the leg, but somehow I made it back to the car and drove away from the scene. They let us get away they didn't even try to follow us either.

I drove everyone to the hospital where T-Money was pronounced dead. The Doctor tried everything to save his life. They took me to another room to patch up the gunshot wound to my leg. I couldn't help but cry when I received the bad news about my best buddy. I promised that whoever did this was going to pay.

Before we had a chance to leave, the police came to question us about the incident, wanting to know who would do this, where it happened at, and other questions we didn't have any answer to.

The police were trying to do their job, but we had to keep it in the street and do our own investigation. After we finished up our business with the police, we drove around everywhere trying to locate that white van. We drove around for hours but didn't have any luck finding them niggas whatsoever.

I told T-Black that he could stay with me and Sergio if he wanted to. That nigga was in a depression shock for three days straight, thinking about the death of his bro. I felt his pain, so I had to reassure him that we were going to find T-Money's killers no matter what it took.

I stayed up for days with no sleep, thinking about my nigga. Seeing as I had no supplier, I had to come up with some type of plan to continue to get this paper. So many thoughts were rushing through my head that I couldn't even think straight. I began to think that maybe it was time for me to get a legit job. Or maybe I could start a business of my own.

As I was sitting and thinking, D-Black walked in.

"I would like to thank you for taking me in," said D-Black. "My brother has a stash of drugs he always told me that if something bad happened to him, to give it to you. He told me that you would look out for me."

"That's really good. Now we can keep your brother's name and dream alive," I replied.

D-Black took me to where the stash spot was, but I became very irate when I saw that it was empty. Damn, someone had beaten us to the punch. At that moment, it became clear that someone had planned to kill T-Money, but I wondered why.

We ransacked the whole place looking for other spots where he might have it hidden, but we didn't have any luck finding anything. Once we gave up the search, T-Money's house phone began to ring. I wondered if I should answer it because I needed to know what the hell was going on. After the fourth ring, I decided to answer.

"Hello," I said.

"Is this Kent'e?" asked an unidentified voice I never heard before.

"Yes, this is him, but who wants to know?" How the hell did he know my name? This seemed too weird how someone would know that we would be here and on top of that, answer the phone.

"I have some information on who killed your friend."

"Really, who was it?"

"I can't give it to you for free. It's going to cost a fee."

"Ok, how much," I asked really wanting to know who would kill my brother by another mother. I can't leave T-Money hanging because he was my friend when no one else wanted to be.

"Pay me ten thousand dollars, I will tell you who they were and where they hang out."

Ten thousand dollars, I thought to myself damn that's a lot of money but hey it's for a cause. How could I trust him when I didn't know this man from Adam? After all, he could be T-Money's killer and now trying to kill me. Still, I had to do it because I needed to learn the truth.

"Okay," I said, *"I can do that. Give me a time and a spot where we can meet.".*

"We could meet at the fish market on 6 Street in the alley. Give me about two hours and by the way come alone and don't try no funny stuff or you would never find out."

"Ok I will meet you in about two hours," I replied before

hanging up the phone.

I was so worried that I might not come home after this meeting. So, I informed Sergio and D-Black on what was about to go down. They insisted on going with me, but I refused because it could become too risky if they came. I also really needed the information because we might be next on the list to get murked.

Two hours later I still had not met the mystery man. Here I was, standing in a dark alley behind the fish market with a briefcase full of money with this half-lit streetlight. I really couldn't see shit, not even my own damn shadow. I jumped when I felt something run past my shoe. It must have been some damn rat. I huffed, feeling very impatient and ready to go.

Before I had the chance to make a move, I heard something moving behind me.

"What the fuck?" I turned around swiftly to see a tall, slender man, dressed in all black, standing right behind me.

I really couldn't make out his face because he was well hidden. *Damn, where did he come from? Is he here to kill me? I cannot believe I just got caught slipping like that.* Paranoia and fear of the unknown can drive anyone crazy.

"I need the cash first," said the raspy voice man.

I slid the briefcase to him. I made sure I didn't make the wrong move because if I did, I knew I was as good as gone. When he opened up the briefcase, I could tell he was happier than a kid in a candy store. When he saw that all the money was accounted for, he handed me a large manila envelope, which contained the info I had been dying to know. Now the wait was finally over.

I slowly opened the envelope, and my jaws dropped when I saw who was in the pictures. I was in total shock that I didn't even notice that the raspy voice man had disappeared.

I left the alley quickly, hurrying so I could meet up with the others. I couldn't wait to spill the beans.

When I told D-Black and Sergio, they couldn't believe what they were hearing. I went over a plan that we were going to do, once we caught the guilty party slipping.

We waited three weeks and on a Friday evening, we put the plan in motion. As we drove up, I spotted three of the niggas I had a fight with in high school. There they were, just sitting in the parking lot of the Waffle House. I started having flashbacks of that day like it just happened yesterday. I already knew how much Dee hated me, especially the fact that T-Money had put me under his wings. That nigga tried to kill me in school and now he has killed my bro. So, this time, it's personal.

I looked at D-Black to let him know it was that time. We put them black goon masks on so no one could recognize us.

Those niggas weren't even paying attention to what was going on, so, D-Black, Sergio, and I snuck up on them. When they finally saw us, I could tell in their faces that they knew they were as good as dead. We had some AKs aiming dead on them so they couldn't make a move. Now look at them in the same position that we were in a couple of weeks ago.

"Why did y'all kill T-Money?" I asked, my face contorted with fury and my eyes locked on my targets.

"He was on a hit list to get taken out," replied Dee, accepting his fate.

A lot of people began to notice the fracas and so jumped in their cars to get away before shit got real. Some others took cover, praying for the best. I couldn't blame them. So many people in the world have been killed by being innocent bystanders.

What type of shit was T-Money in that he would have a bounty on his head? There were so many unanswered questions buzzing in my head and everything seemed mighty fishy.

"Who okayed the hit?" I asked. I was done playing games with these lames.

"I rather die than give you any type of information." His eyes were firm and filled with hatred.

"Ok, if that's how you want to play, then tell the devil in hell, I said what's popping." We just started spraying those niggas with that hot lead. There was a whole lot of screaming and crying going on inside the Waffle House. I walked right up to Dee and shot him five times. His body twitched for that last breath of air and then lay still.

I nodded to the rest and we hurried back to the car so we could get the hell out of there. I took the car to the nearest chop shop and told them to make this car disappear without a trace. One thing I knew for sure was that these hoe ass niggas ain't going to be messing with anyone else again.

"This must be kept a secret...no telling nobody," I said to D-Black and Sergio.

Chapter 9

CHAPTER 9
INOLACHELENNG

Trusting The Untrustworthy

Seeing Kent'e all beaten and messed up by these guys, I couldn't help but be taken down memory lane, as I wondered what decisions I made, led me to this point.

My thoughts took me to my first year at the University of Texas. I was very excited to get away from the high-life environment I grew up in. Yes, I was going to Harvard at first, but I really hated being around all of them stuck-up people. When I left, my parents thought I was making a mistake, passing up on a good education in an Ivy League school, but I let them know I was old enough to make my own decisions.

As a kid growing up, I don't remember going through poverty, but I always heard it on the news. I hated people who didn't even try to better themselves. I believed that there was more to life than doing drugs, gang banging, killing, stealing, prostitution, and staying in the hood for the rest of your life. And don't let me get on the rich and famous people they are no damn better with all their scandals.

I wanted to be different; I wanted to make my own destiny and live my own life. My parents taught my twin brother and me to reach for the stars and never settle for less. I don't even know how the hell my brother Devon turned out the way he did. When we were younger, my parents always gave us what we needed. We didn't have any excuses for getting into trouble. My mother owned two of the top banks in Atlanta and my father owned several businesses. I am very proud of them! They tried every way to help him but nothing seemed to work, so they ended up sending him to Texas to live with our great aunt, hoping that she could change him, but even that didn't work. He became worse off.

Just then, my phone rang and I was shaken out of my thoughts.

"Hello," I said. The only thing I could hear on the other end was crying. "Mom, is that you?"

It was my mother; she finally caught her breath and told me the terrible news that Devon got killed. When she told me that, a part of me died right that instant. I started crying because I hadn't spent any time with him as

I promised him I would. I loved my brother dearly and I just hated he went down the wrong path in life. Everyone told that boy he needed to slow down before he got himself killed or lived the rest of his life in jail. He said he was a grown man so he could do as he pleased.

"It feels like I let him down," my mom said, with so much sadness in her voice. "I gave up on him when in reality he was crying for some help."

"It's not your fault, mom. Everyone makes their own destiny in life. It's either you do good or bad. Everybody knows how much you and Dad loved your kids. Y'all were always there when we needed you. I'm not just going to sit here and let you blame yourself for Devon's actions!"

"I'm going to miss my only son."

"Do the police have any idea about who killed him and why they did it?" I asked.

"No, they do not have any ideas as of yet, but me and your father are giving out a one hundred thousand dollar reward for any information."

I wondered what ever happened to the justice system that we once believed in. It seemed like the crime rate for black-on-black crimes skyrocketed throughout the years. I hope they find the ones who killed my brother and serve justice by giving them life in prison. I wished them to have a slow death instead of a fast one like the death penalty.

I talked to my mother for a long time, and I had never seen her like this before. When she got through expressing her feelings, she hung up the phone. I sat up in my room all night crying and asking God why someone had to take my brother away from me. I wished he could have changed his way before it was too late. The preacher at church always said that things happen for a reason, but I don't understand why it had to happen to me and my family.

The next morning, I woke up early so I could go to the dean's office just to let them know that I needed some time off due to some family emergency. The next morning, I was on a plane to Atlanta so I could face this tragic event along with my family.

My brother's body got shipped back home so everything was ready for us to go to the wake. I had never seen some of these people before in my life, but they seemed as if they loved my brother to death. I walked up to the casket so I could pay my respects. The funeral home did their best with Devon's face due to the fact that the shooters fucked up his face.

I tried to keep my composure, but I couldn't take it anymore. My knees began to tremble and shake. I fell down on my knees, crying, asking God why he had to take my brother away. At that one moment, I made everyone break down and cry. That probably made people think that we were close but in reality, we weren't at all.

When I broke down, my father ran to my side, telling me that everything was going to be okay and that Devon was in a better place now. I hate when people tell me that, knowing damn well nothing was going to be ok.

On the day of the funeral, all the family and friends were there to comfort each other and to pay their respects. After the prayers, I got up to do a little speech to let everyone know that Devon loved and cared about everyone. I talked about getting justice for Devon. When I finished my speech, this R&B group got up to sing the song, "His eye is on the Sparrow." That song was so sad it made everyone get teary eyes. It was a sad, long day.

Once the funeral was over, everyone met at my parent's house for the reception. We had so much food it was more than enough for people to eat.

I went into the room that my mother had fixed up for all my brother's memories. There were pictures of him from a baby up to the age of twelve. Those pictures were way too sad to look at, so I decided to leave that room.

I spent another week at my parent's house. We had so much fun catching up on some lost time. On my last day, I really hated that I had to say goodbye, but I had to get back to school. There was so much work I needed to catch up on.

On my first day back to school, I noticed that my best friend Irene Turner was in my Literature Art class. I didn't even know she got transferred to this school. I remembered the very first time we met she had really pretty brown skin to die for and her hair was down to her waist. We hit it off fast in middle school and have been BFFs ever since! I must admit that she was a beautiful-looking woman, and she got all the attention from the fellas. We did everything together, well almost everything. We never dated the same man, fought, or had sex with each other. I never really thought about dating another woman before but no telling what was on my girl's mind.

One day, when I was in my math class, this sexy dark chocolate man kept staring at me. I couldn't help but smile.

"You know it's not right to stare," I said, still smiling from ear to ear.

"I'm so sorry, Ms. I just couldn't help but notice how beautiful you were. I know it's not polite to stare so if you could please forgive me for that. My name is Tyrone Jackson, and your name is? He reached out his hand for me to shake.

"My name is India Cheyenne," I said as I shook his hand. Damn, his hand felt so manly. It made me wish he could give me a hot oil massage. The thought of that got my panties all wet. I *need to focus my thoughts on something else*, I thought to myself.

"Here is my number," said Tyrone, as he gave me a yellow piece of paper. "So don't be scared to call a brother up."

I'm surprised he didn't ask for mine. *Don't let me find out Mr. Jackson is some kind of gentleman.* I couldn't help but smile.

I just might give you a call one of these days," I said, as

I began fantasizing about Tyrone. I wondered why I felt so sexual about this man. I never felt this way toward any man before.

Tyrone didn't say a word. He just shook his head before I walked out of the room. I wondered what was on his mind. After class I met up with my girl Irene, to tell her all about Tyrone.

"Tyrone? Tyrone who?" asked Irene. Her face was clouded, as though something was troubling her deep inside.

"Tyrone Jackson," I replied.

"Girl, take my advice and run far away. That nigga is a straight-up dog better yet, he is the dog of all dogs, meaning he would fuck anything that walks." Irene sounded alarmed, but I didn't buy it.

It was beginning to look like every time I mentioned some man to Irene, she started telling me some negative BS about them. I concluded that she was just jealous that he never tried to talk to her. *Perhaps, Irene just wants me for herself. Perhaps she is some type of woman lover, because I never see her talking to any man*, I thought to myself.

Irene kept going on and on about how I could get someone better than that dirty dog. She was starting to get on my nerves, so I had to interrupt her.

"What are your plans for the weekend?" I asked, just to change the subject. It was a good thing I did, otherwise, she would have gone on talking and I would have slapped the shit out of her.

"I think we should go pledge for the Delta Sigma Theta just to see if we would make it or not," Irene suggested.

"I think that would be a great idea," I said. *Lord knows we might just make it.*

That night as I laid in bed, I couldn't help but think about my new chocolate drop friend. I decided that I wasn't going to rush just yet. I had to get to know him before I made any decisions.

***

Everything was going so well with me and Tyrone being friends, but Irene couldn't stand the thought of me and him being friends. I could feel the jealousy in her voice when she talked shit about him. That shit was starting to get on my nerves, so I started ignoring her. She looked at me and got the picture that I didn't want to hear that BS no more.

"You are going to be sorry. Watch and see," Irene said.

"Whatever you say, jealous ass bitch," I said under my breath so Irene really couldn't hear it.

Tyrone took me on a couple of dates. We were hitting it off so well. It was as if we were made for each other, because not once did he ask for the booty like most men would do. He told me all about his hopes and dreams and how he was thinking about going to the police academy in Dallas.

"I think you should go for what makes you happy," I said to him.

"I want to but...." Tyrone started to say but stopped.

"But what, Tyrone." I was so curious about what he was going to say next.

"I know we have been friends for a while, but I don't want to lose you to another man," he said, staring into my eyes.

"Tyrone, you are so sweet, You really know how to get a girl's attention for real." My face lit up with a bright red blush.

"So, can you tell me one thing," he said, contemplating what he would say next.

"Would you do the honor of being the special lady in my life?" he finally asked.

"What are you trying to ask me, Tyrone?"

Tyrone got down on one knee and pulled out a big diamond ring. *Damn, am I dreaming or something because this seems unreal?* I was beyond shocked.

"I know I don't know you well, but I would love to make you my woman," he said, looking up at me with those eyes.

"Wow! That's kind of fast, don't you think," I said, trying to keep my emotions in check.

While on his knees, he started begging like Keith Sweet until I gave in and said yes.

"Yes, it would be an honor to be your woman," I said,

as tears started rolling down my face. It was the happiest feeling I ever had.

When I said the answer Tyrone wanted to hear, he gave me one of the most passionate kisses that I ever experienced in my whole life. I could feel the moisture in my vagina, as its walls quaked and ached for some deep loving. I had said yes because he begged me to and he made me feel good, but I still had a sense of foreboding. *I hope I know what I'm getting myself into by accepting this proposal of being his woman.*

Although I had doubts, I still wanted Tyrone. Tyrone was the kind of man who listened to everything I said. I remember when I was talking to him about my desire to own my own business one day. He was supportive of the idea.

"Don't ever give up on your dreams," said Tyrone. "Whatever you want out of life, reach for the stars."

Tyrone reminded me so much of my father. They both were passionate as hell. Every time I was with Tyrone, I just wanted to give him all of my love. I often wondered why I felt so highly about him. I hoped that he felt as strongly as I felt for him.

The next day I went to class, and it seemed as if everyone was staring at me. There was this yellow bitch staring too hard so I knew it couldn't be because of my glowing skin. They called her Lisa and I was getting pissed by her hard stares.

"What the hell are you staring at?" I asked.

"Why the hell are you sleeping with my man bitch," said Lisa.

I sat there for a moment looking all puzzled, trying to figure out what the hell this broad was talking about.

"What man are you talking about?"

"You know who I am talking about bitch. Don't act dumb.

If this high yellow broad call me a bitch one more time I'm going to slap her, I thought, clenching and unclenching my fist.

I began to wonder if she was referring to my chocolate drop Tyrone. So, I blurted out, "Bitch, Tyrone ain't yours. He asked me to be his woman and I said yes."

"Who are you calling a bitch? Lisa asked. "You are the bitch for sleeping with a nigga you ain't even known that long."

Everyone in the class was having a ball with this one.

This hoe better shut up before she makes me snatch off her ugly ass wig.

"Hey, ladies, quiet down. You are distracting the other students," Professor Peabody said.

I just ignored the Professor and said, "First of all, I never slept with Tyrone or anyone else at this school."

"That ain't what I heard bitch," she said, as she slapped the shit out of me. I could tell it was a hard slap because I could feel the print on my face. I zoned out for a little bit, but I could still hear the words, *fight, fight, fight* in the background. At that very moment, I knew what I had to do. Everyone started getting up to see what was going to happen next. That bitch got me fucked up if she thought that I was just going to accept that.

I jumped up and said, "You done fucked up now."

She tried to fight me when she saw that it just got real up in here. When she swung, she missed so I caught her in the face with a two-piece special. By the look on her face, I could tell that she was in a daze but that didn't stop me from tagging that ass some more. When she hit the floor, I ran up and grabbed her by her nappy ass weave. I hope she doesn't think I was done with her ass just yet.

Everybody was so crunked in my class as they kept screaming and hollering. I can't even remember what all I had done to the bitch because I was fired up. But what I do remember is the police breaking us up and taking us to the dean's office.

Dean Mahogany was pissed at us for acting like little kids. She gave us a lecture on how we should be role models for our peers. She also warned that if another incident like this ever happened again, she would expel us and ensure we never got into another university.

"I am letting the both of you off the hook, just this one time, only because I am friends with both of your moms, do this again there won't be another chance," said Dean Mahogany.

I took one look into her eyes and could tell that she was not playing any games.

"But don't just think that I'm letting the both of you off the hook this easy. There still has to be some type of punishment for disrespecting your classmates. So after class, for two weeks, I want both of you to do some extra duty work. Do I make myself clear?" the dean asked.

"Yes Ma'am," the both of us said.

"Are there going to be any more problems between you two, if it is let me know now so we can just skip to phase two and kick you out for the rest of the semester."

"No, no I don't want that, India said, I promise you that I'm going to keep myself out of trouble."

"Right, I can't afford to drop any of my classes so I'm a get some act right," said Lisa.

I began to wonder if Tyrone was going around telling people he slept with me. Well anyway, I knew that bitch ass Lisa was going to remember that ass whopping she got from me. So that bitch was going to be the last person I had to worry about.

Two weeks after that incident I still didn't confront Tyrone for lying on me. That nigga had some nerve-making allegations about our invisible sex life. I called him up so I could give him a piece of my mind. He was over there laughing at me I hate when people do that shit.

"That shit isn't funny," I said. "I almost got kicked out of school because of your ass."

"Baby, don't sweat that shit. She is just mad because I'm with you," Tyrone clarified. "I don't even know what I saw in her."

I went on with my story, telling him how I caught her with a two-piece special then pulled out her nappy ass hair. *Ole dirty head ass bitch* just the thought of that fight made me mad all over again. He was laughing so loud I had to move the phone off my ear.

"Are you coming to spend some time with me later on tonight? "Tyrone asked, in his sexy voice.

"I really want to, but I have a whole lot of work I need to catch up on."

"Ok, baby. I guess I'll talk to you tomorrow; I love you a long time."

Hahaha, I guffawed. "I love you too boo," I said, before hanging up the phone. There's never a dull moment with that man.

As soon as I got off the phone, I got started on my work so I could be caught up on everything. If I get through on time, I might surprise him with a little visit to his dorm room. When I got finished, I decided to give him a call, but he didn't answer his phone. I wondered where his ass was at. It was not like him not to answer my call. Maybe he was in a deep sleep, but I already knew that he would wake up for me when I made it over there.

When I got to his door, I could hear some kind of noise that got louder and louder. My heart dropped fifty feet below. I could sense fear coiling inside of me. Something was not right.

Snap out of it India, I thought to myself. I tried the door just to see if it was unlocked and what did I see? Another bitch riding on my man, but how stupid can a person be not to lock the door.

"Oh hell Naw, I know that bitch didn't," I said, before dropping my purse to the floor.

There Tyrone was, having sex with that Lisa bitch. They both looked at me when they heard my voice. That bitch had some big balls to smile at me, damn how I wished I could put my feet so deep up in her ass, but I couldn't because I didn't want to get kicked out of school.

"India, I am very sorry," Tyrone said, as he started putting on his clothes. "I was going to tell her that it was over between me and her, but it ended up like this. Lisa doesn't mean shit to me, I promise you that. She was just a nut to get off."

Damn, that was harsh as fuck, but at least that smile she had turned into a frown. Lisa got out the bed so she could get dressed as soon as she was done, she slapped the shit out of Tyrone. His ear must have rung.

"Why did you tell me that India wasn't shit to you and how you wanted to please me in every way you can imagine? I can't believe you used me for sex," Lisa said, as she slapped him a second time.

She tried to slap him again until he grabbed her arm and

pushed her on the floor. "You better get out of here before I hurt you." She got up and ran off crying.

I was just looking, trying to see what was about to happen next. I didn't feel sorry for his ass that's what he gets, trying to have two women at the same time. I can't believe Tyrone lied about everything. I felt so sorry for her because I could look her in the eyes and tell that she really loved him. I gave it some thought by taking off the ring that he gave me and gave it right back to his trifling ass.

"I am very sorry that this happened," Tyrone said with teary eyes. "I didn't mean for it to happen this way."

"Tyrone it's over," I said, trying not to shed a tear. "I don't want to be with you anymore."

I was scarred deeply I couldn't even stand seeing his face, because I might have hurt him for real.

"Baby don't say that. We can work this out together."

"I don't think we can," I said, as I ran away from him.

"India, please let me make it up to you," Tyrone screamed out loud.

I just ignored his ass and kept on stepping, so I could be alone. I guess his dog ass got the picture because he wasn't trailing behind me anymore. I don't even know why I was so stupid to believe in him in the first place. If I had listened to Irene when she told me about him, I wouldn't be in this mess now.

I went to sit by a corner, nursing my broken heart. I bet everyone and their momma had heard the news, and

I knew Irene's ass was over there laughing up a storm, saying, *I told that girl*. I wanted to pick up the phone to call up my mother to tell her what happened but I really didn't want to talk to anyone at the moment. So, I just went to my room to sleep.

Chapter 10

Close Calls and Consequences

It was a hot and sunny day, and I decided that I wanted to go play a little b-ball at the park. It has been a very long time since I played the sport, and it was obvious that I wasn't in the best shape as I once was. There I was, panting, trying to keep up but one damn thing I knew for sure was that none of these niggas can't fuck with me.

I was getting tired of this one nigga that was guarding me. It seemed like every time I got the ball, he would foul me. He really was pissing me off. I wasn't going to say anything, but he kept on like he was doing it on purpose.

"Why the fuck do you keep fouling me?" I asked. "We ain't playing no damn football."

"Nigga, don't get mad because your bitch ass doesn't

have no skills," said the dude.

"If I didn't have no skills, how come I keep crossing you up?" I fired back.

"Phsss, nigga please."

"Yea nigga, don't hate," I said, as I dribbled the ball through his legs. "And if you foul me one more time, watch what's going to happen next. Believe that."

"Nigga, you just bumping your lips. I'm known for exposing cowards like you."

This nigga must not know who the fuck I am, I thought out loud to myself.

Oh, hell naw this nigga is fouling me on purpose. This is the last straw. I told someone that was standing on the sideline to come to take my spot and that I would be right back. I went to my car picked up my burner and put it on the side of my hip. I made it back to the basketball court like nothing was bothering me.

"Nigga, I told you that if you foul me one more time, something was going to happen to you," I said, holding my composure.

"I'd whoop your bitch ass little nigga," the dude said, as he took his shirt off.

I must admit the dude was huge as fuck, but I guess he thought a gangsta was supposed to be scared of him or something. He kept barking off at the mouth, talking about how he is not like none of these other niggas on this court.

"Nigga you are so right," I said, as I took out my burner and hit him smooth across the head.

That nigga's eyes got big as fuck when I did that. I could tell he wanted to run but instead, his big ass hit the pavement on the court. I was so mad because I was having a good day until he pushed the wrong buttons. I don't have an on or off switch because I wasn't made that way.

"Nigga, you must think I'm a punk," I said, ready to shoot him as he lay on the floor.

Everyone kept their distance just in case bullets started flying.

"Please don't shoot me," the coward pleaded. "I apologize for disrespecting you like that."

I couldn't believe that this was the same nigga that everyone was afraid of. This ole Debo-looking ass nigga was softer than a box of Charmin tissue. I know he wasn't scared of anybody, but I do know he was afraid that I got the upper hand on his ass.

"Listen up nigga, I'm going to let you make it today," I said, as I put my burner away. "I swear to God if this shit ever happens again you will get plucked."

"Yes, sir it won't happen again," he said, as he picked himself up off the ground and got in a car with some big booty woman.

As I looked up, I saw Sergio and D-Black standing behind me with their burners out, ready to shoot anyone who thought of making the wrong move.

I wonder where they came from. They weren't here at first, I thought to myself.

"Bitch ass niggas, don't be sneaking up on me like that. I almost murked the both of y'all.

"Damn, bro! What the fuck happened over here," asked Sergio. We were across the street hollering at the ladies when we saw you go to your car to get your burner."

"Man, I was about to shoot this mark ass nigga because he kept barking up the wrong tree with all that bumping. I told him time and time again to stop fouling me, but he kept on. I guess he thought I was bullshitting when I said I was going to get on his ass if he kept on," I told them.

"Nigga, you are crazy," D-Black said, laughing his ass off.

We were out there acting an ass, as we were walking towards my car. In the background, I could hear somebody screaming, "Nigga, let me holla at you right quick."

My heart started beating a hundred beats per hour, as I wondered if he had come back for me. *Was it my time to get erased from this earth?*

Rule number one everyone can be touched, so don't think you are Superman. So, I turned around with my hand on the butt of my strap, awaiting my fate, but it wasn't him. It was some other dude ten times his size. I prayed to God hoping we didn't have to hurt this nigga. I could already feel the tension from the way Sergio and D-Black were looking.

"What do you want nigga?" I asked, sizing him up and

down.

"I didn't come for no trouble. My name is Antwon Tuck, but people call me Tu-Tank and I was wondering if I could join your little clique."

"Wtf! We ain't no muthafuckan gang members," said Sergio with a sarcastic grin. "We make money over here."

"I can be loyal. Just give me a chance to prove myself to you. I would be there to back you up no matter what."

I could tell that he was sincere and brave to come to me seeking a proposition. That's what I love about that young nigga. Dedication.

"Maybe I should start up a clique of mob niggas so we can rule the world," I thought to myself.

I had to really think about this. I came up with one of the quickest conclusions ever. I felt like I could put Tu-Tank to good use.

"Come on nigga," I said. "You can roll with the big dawgs." That nigga looked so happy, just to be part of the family.

Weeks passed since I let Tu-Tank in. We learned so much about his life. His real name was Antwon Tuck, aged 18, born in Chicago aka Chiraq, but raised in Texas. He had two older brothers that were deep in the dope game. He told us about how they got killed in a shootout with some crooked ass cops. I really felt sorry for him because my family and I went through the same thing with our parents' death.

The streets were hot as fuck due to the elections, so we couldn't frolic the streets like we wanted to. Besides, the feds were still watching us. That night I came up with a plan that would make us some money. I asked them what they thought about the plan.

"I think we should go for it," Sergio suggested.

My brother always liked doing something illegal, I thought to myself.

"Is it going to be one of those little banks or one of those big city banks, asked D-Black?"

"I think we could start with one of those medium banks first," I said.

"Who is going to be the getaway driver?" Tu-Tank asked me.

"You can have the job, but only if you can handle it," I replied.

"I don't mind doing it. I believe I can handle it with no problem."

"Ok, now that's settled. Let's take an oath that if one of us gets caught, we won't snitch on our brothers."

Everyone obliged me and took the oath.

"Ok, listen up everyone, this isn't going to be an easy task, but it can be done if we stick to the plan. Once you are in, there is no turning back. I'm about to send each one of y'all on a mission that I need y'all to complete."

First, I sent Sergio to scope out the bank in downtown Dallas and make a report on the ins and outs of the place.

Next, I gave D-Black a list of disguises to pick up at Party City. It was some good disguises so people wouldn't be able to give a good description of our appearance. I also wanted him to pick up some type of glue so our fingerprints wouldn't show up on anything we touched. Last but not least, I sent Tu-Tank to get two types of getaway cars. One was to get there and the other was to get away. I also sent myself on a task to get some new firearms from my plug. I don't know why I'm so obsessed with guns.

It took us two weeks to get the plan down pat so there won't be any mistakes made. When we made it to the bank, I waited for Sergio and Tu-Tank to go in, and then I followed suit behind them. I waited in line with my disguise on, watching the hand on my watch move.

It was almost time so I walked out of line. I waited for the two guards to come out of the safe with six big bags of cash.

I snuck up behind them and said, "Don't make the wrong move or I'm a blow your heads off." I took their guns away from them for their safety.

"EVERYBODY ON THE MUTHAFUCKAN FLOOR," Sergio screamed out.

"What the hell are you looking at?" D-Black said as he kicks the shit out of some man in a dark blue shirt.

He made his way toward the three bank tellers who were on duty and pulled out the gray electric tape. "If you want to keep breathing, then you need to put your hands behind your backs."

"Everybody listen up," I said. "Everyone stay on the ground and you won't get hurt, but if you want to do a Superman act, you are going to pay for it. Believe that."

We had about five minutes before the police came, so we needed to hurry up. D-Black and I began putting all the money in the trash bags that we brought in. We were halfway out the door when this one police officer came from around the corner with his gun out and shot D-Black in the ass. My nigga screamed out loud "fuck" when that bullet hit his skin, but not once did he let go of that bag. Sergio turned around so fast and shot the pig ten times, nine times in his body and one time in the head. Everybody in the bank started screaming when they saw the cop drop like a fly, his blood spattered on the floor when his body hit the floor.

Damn, it wasn't supposed to go like this, the whole plan was to get the money and get the hell out and not to hurt anyone, but that pig had to come out and fuck that up.

"Come on niggas, let's get the fuck up out of here before some more pigs show up," I screamed.

I really didn't feel like dying that day, so I grabbed two bags, Sergio grabbed two and said "fuck them other two bags." Damn, these bags were heavy as fuck, but we still managed to carry them out. Tu-Tank saw us running out of the bank he hurried up and scoop us up after he saw that D-Black was holding his ass.

"Damn that was a close one," said Sergio, laughing up a storm.

"Nigga, that shit isn't funny. I got shot in my ass in there," D-Black said. I could have died in there but thank God you were there for me."

"D-Black, are you ok fam," I asked, looking back and making sure no one was following us.

"Yeah, I'm a be ok, I still can't believe that muthafucka shot me in the ass though."

I wondered how much money we came up on but we would have to wait until we got to the spot. As I was sitting there thinking to myself how crazy this was, I could hear police sirens in the background.

"Tu-Tank, I think you need to step on it because it sounds like them hoes are getting closer," I suggested.

"Aight, I gotcha, said Tu-Tank, as he smashed on the gas a little faster.

Damn, this shit can't be happening. Just when my life started getting better, the worst was coming full throttle. I looked back and saw a police car behind us with its lights flashing for us to pull over.

"Fuck, there is a cop car behind us," I said nervously. "Y'all don't get all nervous and look suspicious maybe they will pass us by.

I had a feeling that we should have never tried to do something new, but hey it was my idea so if we got pulled over, I decided I would take the charge. With all this cash we are looking at big fed time. I swore to God that if we got out of this mess in one piece, I wouldn't ever do this again. As soon as I peeped around to see if they were still tailing us, they kept flashing their lights.

"What the fuck did I do that for?" I said under my breath.

"Pull this car over now," one of the policemen said, over the loudspeaker.

"King, do you want me to pull over or smash the gas to try to lose them again?" asked Tu-Tank.

"Yeah, go on and pull over so we don't make the situation worse than it already is. The last thing we need is for the cops to open fire on us. I'm so glad we put the loot and the disguises in the trunk.

"Put your hands up where I can see them," one of the policemen said, as he walked towards the car with his gun in his hands.

"This doesn't look so good," said Sergio.

The policeman asked Tu-Tank for his license and registration. He took it and looked at it closely.

"Why were you going over the speed limit?" asked the other officer, chewing on some tobacco.

I said the first thing that came to my mind. "We were in a hurry to get to the hospital because my grandmother was in a bad accident."

"Do y'all have anything in the car that we should know about?" asked the officer holding Tu-Tank's ID.

My heart dropped a little when he asked that. My first thought was to pick up my strap on the side of me and do them both in. It was a good thing that they received a call for backup.

"Here you go," said the police, as he handed Tu-Tank back his fake ID. "I'm going to let you make it this one time because you were trying to get to your grandmother but if I catch you speeding again, there are going to be consequences. Do I make myself clear, son?

"Yes, sir," we chorused.

"Damn! That was a close one," I said, as soon I saw the laws were out of sight. "Well, I know one damn thing for sure, this shit ain't never going to happen again. I don't know about y'all niggas, but I was scared as fuck."

I could tell that my crew was scared shitless by the expression on their faces. We hurried up to where our other car was parked, so we could ditch the car we had done the crime in. After we got out of the car with our loot, I took a match and gasoline and set that bitch on fire.

I was sure glad when we made it to the spot in one piece because it could have gone south. Thank the Lord for watching over us. Once we made it to the door, we dumped all the cash on the floor. My eyes got big when I saw how much cash we got away with. Five hundred thousand dollars all in one-hundred-dollar bills. I guess it was worth it, but I prayed that the death of that police didn't come back to bite us in the ass.

Chapter 11

Same Old Story

Life seems at its best until you come upon a crazy situation to make you rethink about your life.

Two years after I called it off with Tyrone, I was still missing him. All I wanted to do was pick up the phone and hear his voice. That man had one of the deepest voices I ever heard. Just him saying hello got me wet. I don't even know why I was thinking about his ass so much when he was the one that cheated on me. I never grew up having a boyfriend because my dad wasn't too thrilled with his baby girl growing up too fast. I still heard the sound of his voice telling me, "Baby girl, some men ain't shit, so watch who you have soul ties with."

Tyrone was the first man I truly gave my heart to; I

wondered what made him so special. As I sat there trying to get my mind right, the cell phone rang.

RRIIIINNNNGGG! RRIIINNNNGG! RRIIIN-NNGG!

I sat there for a minute wondering who was calling me because I had never seen this number before. *I guess I will answer just to see who it is.*

"Hello," I said, listening and trying to catch the voice on the other end.

"Hi sweetie, how are you?" Tyrone said, in a deep voice.

Damn, I was just thinking about him he must have a tracking device on my mind or something. I need to play it cool so he wouldn't think that I'm still mad at him.

"What the hell do you want, Tyrone?"

"Damn! I can't get a hello or a fuck you back? Well anyway, I gave it some thought I was wrong as hell for treating you the way I have done. I hope you can dig deep down in your heart to forgive me for all my wrongs."

"I don't know if I can do that."

"I promise you that things will be a whole lot different this time around."

I sighed. "What made you call me?" I asked. "Because I really don't think I could ever trust you again."

"I wanted to show you that I am for real this time," said Tyrone. "Do you think we can go somewhere special so we can sit down and talk about it?"

"I guess we can, but no funny business mister or you

might get socked in the eye."

"Okay," said Tyrone, giggling. "I will be there to pick you up a seven so be ready."

I wonder where we are going that is so special, India thought to herself.

"Well, I guess I will see you when I see you," I said, before hanging up the phone. I didn't even give him a chance to say anything else.

I decided I would not tell Irene that I was going to go meet up with Tyrone, because Lord knows I didn't want to hear her bitching and complaining to me.

It was a quarter after seven when I was standing outside, waiting on Tyrone to show up. Then this fine sexy man approached me.

"Hey Ma," said the stranger. "I hope I'm not intruding."

"No, you are not, just wondering what the hell you want," I said, rolling my eyes, already a bit pissed that Tyrone was keeping me waiting.

"I just wanted to say damn, you are fine as hell, looking like one of those top-grade models that came off the cover of a King Magazine," he said, charm dripping all over him.

And of course, I could not resist his charm, because what he was saying got me smiling from ear to ear. "Thank you very much. I'm just waiting on a friend to come pick me."

"Do you think it would be wrong of me to ask you for your number, so I call you up sometime?" asked the stranger as he pulled out his cell phone.

I folded my arms and looked at him as if he was crazy. "I'm not about to give a complete stranger my number. I don't even know your name so how can you just approach me and ask me for my number?"

He chuckled. "My name is Chris, and the reason I didn't tell you is because you never asked for it. Can you tell me your name, Ma?"

"My name is India, not Ma. Do you think I could get your number instead?"

"Whatever floats your boat?"

After he gave me his number, we said our goodbyes, but deep down inside I was hoping we never crossed paths again. Or did I? Because, fuck he did look good, and I would love to give him a taste of this milkshake.

I looked up in time to see Tyrone had made it. I snapped out of my deviant fantasy about my new friend. *Oh God! I wonder how long he has been here waiting on me. Did he see me talking to Chris?*

When I got in the car, it was quiet as hell. It was so quiet I could hear a pin drop on the floor. I looked over at him and I could tell that something was bothering him. I guess he couldn't make do with the silence, as he spoke up.

"Who was that nigga you were talking to?" Tyrone asked.

"I don't have to explain myself to you. The last time I checked, I was single," I stated plainly.

"Whatever you say, India."

When I said those words, he shut the hell up but I could tell that he was angry and hurt at the same time.

"Where are you taking me?" I asked.

"You will see once we get there so sit back and enjoy the ride," he said, with a smile on his face.

I was relieved that Tyrone did not press further about the situation with Chris, because I just didn't want to talk about it.

"What is the special occasion?" I asked, looking around.

"Well, in two weeks, I would be graduating from the police academy, and I wanted to sit down and spend some time with you," he replied.

"Whatever." India sighed.

"I am being so for real India," Tyrone said. "I have grown over these few years. I know what I did was unforgivable, but please tell me you are not going to hate me for the rest of your life."

Damn! I couldn't believe he was trying to make me feel guilty and it was working. I felt so bad for treating him this way. I couldn't even congratulate him.

"The only way I will forgive you is if you promise me that you would never ever do anything like this again."

"I promise that I would be your knight in shining armor, and I promise to never hurt you again."

We pulled up at one of the finest high-class restaurants located in downtown Dallas. I couldn't believe my eyes about how many cars were parked in the parking lot.

"Are you sure you can afford this place," I asked. "If not, I don't mind eating somewhere else?"

"Don't worry about anything. I got this," Tyrone said.

"Oh ok." I didn't want to step on anyone's toes, but I couldn't help but wonder where Tyrone got all this money to afford a place like this. I prayed to God that he wasn't doing anything illegal. *Good Lord, it was 100 dollars just to park VIP.*

When we walked into the building, everything looked very high maintenance. There were chandeliers hanging everywhere. I bet they spent over a million dollars on this place. I know high class when I see it. I was born and raised in a very wealthy family, but I was taught never to waste my money on anything that doesn't serve a purpose in life.

When we got to our table it was well organized and decorated well. When we set down at our table, I picked up one of the menus just to see what they had. *Damn, this food is costly as hell,* I screamed inwardly because the cheapest thing on this menu was seventy dollars and that was a bitch ass salad.

"Just to let you know that you can order anything you want," Tyrone said as he looked over his menu.

Tyrone decided to order a 12-ounce Wagyu beef with asparagus and buttered potatoes which cost about three hundred and fifty dollars. The only thing I could order was shrimp salad with avocado and a glass of wine. I really didn't want anything else because the prices were too damn high, who in the hell would buy a lobster frittata for one thousand dollars, and what the hell is a frittata? Tyrone was fussing at me, asking me why I didn't get what I really wanted? The only answer I could come up with was that I wasn't really hungry.

After we finished eating, I ordered the Golden Sundae with Madagascar vanilla beans, topped with 23K edible gold leaves, sprinkled with a couple of expensive rare chocolates. I liked the fact that it was served in a gold goblet with an 18-carat spoon. This was one of the best thousand-dollar Sundae that I ever had in my life.

We sat there for half an hour just talking about what was going on in our lives over these last couple of years. As soon as we finished our little chat, Tyrone drove me back home.

"I would like to thank you for the lovely evening," I said.

"I'm glad you enjoyed yourself, but do you think I can come in so we can talk for a couple of minutes," asked Tyrone.

"Hmmm, I don't think that would be such a good idea. You know that Irene hates your guts so I will talk to you tomorrow."

Damn! I wished I could get some deep loving from him.

"Do you promise to give me a call, my cutie pie?" asked Tyrone, as he gave me a nice tight hug.

"I promise I will, my sweet teddy bear," I said as I gave him a big kiss good night.

I held him so tight because I wasn't ready to let him go just yet. We finally separated and he left, while I went in. As soon as I walked in, there Irene was, sitting on the couch watching the movie "Think Like a Man."

"Girl, where the hell have you been? I been worried about you all night," said Irene as she turned the sound down.

"I'm so sorry I didn't call to let you know that I was okay. I went on a very nice dinner date with a special someone."

"Do you mind telling me with whom?" Her eyes never left my face as she looked me deep into my eyes.

Damn, I knew that she was going to ask me that question. The way she looked at me was like she already knew with who. I had to think of a fake name quickly.

"I caught up with one of my male friends from high school," I said, blushing.

"I can tell that you had a really good time," Irene replied, throwing a pillow at me.

"Yeah, girl, I did. He took me to the Dajorian Restaurant in Downtown Dallas. There were some many people that we really didn't find a place to park."

"Damn, you must got yourself a baller to take you to a place like that. I always dreamed of visiting there one of these days. So tell me about it."

"It was one of the best experiences I have ever had in my whole life. Everything in there was well decorated and the price was high as hell. Can you believe a damn salad was seventy dollars?"

"Damn, for a damn salad?"

"Girl, that's not all. They have this Lobster called the Zillion Dollar Lobster Frittata topped with 10 ounces of caviar and that bitch is $1000 by itself."

Irene's eyes got wide when she heard the word one thousand dollars. She said, "Well, so are you going to see him again?"

"Do you think I should?"

"I say go for what you want, but are you sure he ain't no damn drug dealer?"

"Dear God, I sure hope not." I laughed out loud. "That would be the death of me if he was. I'm not trying to be no Queen Pin."

"Girl you are so silly. I say get that man."

Irene and I burst out laughing about that. We sat up and talked for a while until she said that she was about to call it a night because she had a long day ahead of her.

I wasn't tired just yet, so I relaxed in my room bored as fuck, watching reruns of Living Single. I had enough of this shit, so I picked up my iPhone to call my new friend to see if he was up.

"Hello, who is this?" asked Chris.

I guess he was having a party or something because it was too loud, and I could barely hear him.

"Hey stranger, do you know who this is?" I asked, trying to play with his mind.

"Is this my new friend, India?"

"Yes, this is the one that was on the cover of the King Magazine," I said with a giggle. "Did I catch you at a really bad time, because you sound busy?"

"Naw, you good, I was hoping you would give me a call. I'm not doing too much of anything, just sipping on some good wine at this party my roomie decided to throw over here. You can come over if you like to."

"I guess I can do that since I'm not doing anything spectacular at the moment."

"Oh, ok that's what's up. I'm texting you the address right now so you can find it."

"Ok, Hun. I'm a see you in a few."

When I went over there, I saw there were a lot of people dancing outside. All I could hear in the background was, *you ain't nothing but a hoochie mama! Hood rat, Hood rat hoochie mama!* When I walked in, it was so crowded, I could barely move. Some people just don't have any manners they kept bumping into me without saying, *excuse me*. I didn't know where Chris was, but he spotted me from across the room and he could tell how frustrated I was.

"Hey Ma, I didn't think you were going to show up for real," said Chris, as he gave me a hug.

"I was really trying to make up my mind if I really wanted to come or not."

"Well, I'm really glad you decided to come."

"Me too," I said, grinning from ear to ear.

"Do you want to go sit on the couch in the den so we can talk?"

"Yes, we can do that because my legs are killing me."

As we sat there having one of the greatest conversations ever, one of Chris's friends approached him asking if he wanted some candy. I'm over there wondering what kind of candy he was talking about because I heard of people eating edible weed brownies and cookies. I almost lost it when he started snorting drugs right in front of me like I wasn't there. Not trying to be a bitch, but I hated partying with people who do drugs and it seemed as if everyone in here was on something. I wanted to leave so bad, but I couldn't get my nerves built up to walk out the door.

Chris looked over at me with the most embarrassing face ever.

"Do you want to try some of this?" Chris asked me as he snorted another line of coke.

I wanted to slap the shit out of him just for asking me that question. "I don't want to do anything that's going to hurt me," I said, looking for the nearest exit.

"I wouldn't give you anything that would hurt you, Ma. Does it look like there's anything wrong with me?"

"No, you look healthier than a pro basketball player."

"Well, just try a little just to see if you like it or not."

"Ok, I guess I could try just a little," I said as I picked up a rolled-up twenty-dollar bill and snorted a half line. It wasn't like I thought it was going to be, so I don't know why I was so scared of the unthinkable.

After another hit and a shot of liquor, I was space-age pimpin' like Eightball & MJG. I was up dancing when it hit me hard. *Damn, what's happening to me.* Everything in my body was getting numb. My head started spinning faster than a spinning top and now my vision was getting blurry by the minute. I needed to lie down for a minute or two until it wore off. As soon as I laid down on the couch I passed the fuck out, lost in my head and oblivious about what was going to happen to me. *Why am I so stupid? Why the fuck did I even listen to this asshole for?*

The next morning, I woke up throwing up everywhere, my nose still stopped up and noticed I was naked, under a thin sheet. What the fuck happened? I didn't feel any-thing, but I feel like I'd been raped. I looked around to see who was in the room with me. There Chris was, passed out on the loveseat, naked as well, his meat just hanging out with a condom still on it. Seeing that shit brought my spirit all the way down as I realized that he took advantage of me.

I stood up so I could scramble all my things off the floor. I hurried up and got dressed so I could sneak out without making a sound. I was halfway out the door when I heard him call my name. I was so scared I wasn't trying to stay in here another moment with this rapist.

"What's wrong, Ma?" asked Chris.

"What's wrong, really? Nigga you raped me that's what's wrong with me," I said as tears began to flow.

"You took advantage of me; you knew what that shit was going to do to me. I don't even know why I trusted him in the first place. " I was so furious with hate I slapped the shit out of him not worrying about the consequences of doing so.

"I deserve that," Chris said. "Do you think we can start over? We started on the wrong foot."

I looked at that nigga like he done lost his damn mind. What the hell is wrong with these men nowadays?

"Hell to the naw, nigga. I don't ever want to see your ugly ass face again and if you ever approach me in any form or fashion, I will call the police on you."

"But... but," he stuttered, as he tried to stop me from leaving out the door.

"And if I don't make it home at all, my best friend was warned to call the police. She is aware of my whereabouts," I lied. He let me go then.

I was so mad when I stormed out. *Why Lord, why do I have to keep meeting all the wrong men?* I prayed that one day I would find my Mr. Right, but until that day came, I would give Tyrone another chance. I really wanted to press charges on Chris, but I knew the police ain't going to do shit about it, so I needed to ease my mind and come up with another plan to get even.

Chapter 12

A Clash of Colors and New Allies

I remember growing up back in the day when there were no such things as Bloods, Crips, Vice Lords, Folks, or Latin Kings in my hood. Now the whole world was infected with all types of different organizations. I already knew that California was the birthplace of the Bloods and Crips. When I first saw how the Bloods were, I became very obsessed with their style. But what really caught my eye the most was they were really hungry when it came to that bread, so from then on red had been one of my favorite colors.

Every time I hung around them, they always wanted to put me down with their set, but my mom wasn't having that shit. I wasn't the type of person who liked to be told what to do and when to do it. I never had to prove myself to anyone because all my niggas already know that I would ride and die with them no matter what. I never discriminated against anyone, as I had a couple of friends who were Crips, so I didn't really have beef with them.

In the early '90s, I heard that Bloods and Crips hated each other to the fullest. At that time, Fort Worth was a murderous city. Every time I went to school, one of my friends ended up dying. It was very sad knowing that Black people were dying over a color. I always wanted to put together a peace treaty, but no one wanted to act right.

When I drove past the supermarket in my old neighborhood, there were a bunch of niggas dressed in red standing in front of the hood store. One of them looked just like my relative, Mo Blood. The last time I saw him, he was just a YG. I got out of the car and approached the group of men. Mo was flamed up with a white tee, red dickies, and some all-red 11 Jordans.

"What's poppin', dawg? I asked.

"Shit, nothing, Blood, just trying to stack this paper up. Where are your crazy ass brother and sister at?"

"Ki is in college. She goes to Spelman in Atlanta Georgia, and I don't know where Sergio at. Come to think of it, half the time I don't know where his ass at."

"Lol, damn! Your bro be wildin' out fam. Have the police found any leads on the death of your parents? "Asked Mo, as he took a puff of a blunt.

"No, but I wish I could find out who did it," I said, as I saw an all-black Regal with dark-tinted windows, pulling in front of the hood store.

"I looked at, Mo, is that some more of your homies that just pulled up?"

"Hell, naw fam. I don't know who the hell that is. I've never seen that car before."

As soon as he said that, three dudes jumped out, with masks on their faces, and burners in their hands, and just started busting. When the people on the inside and outside the store saw what was going on, some screamed, ducked and some even tried to get away from all this madness. *Shit!*

I'm no Superman, so I hid behind the vehicle that was in front of me. I felt so helpless because I left my heat in the car and there was nothing I could really do. Three steps in front of me, two of Mo's homeboys were in their own puddle of blood and just lifeless. When they saw that their niggas were hit, they started busting back. The three masked me jumped in the car when they saw that some more Bloods were coming from around the corner.

"Lookout fam," Mo said. "I'm a bark at you at another time because I'm about to go murk me some niggas."

"Aiiight my nigga it was really nice seeing you again, Fam," I said.

"Me too, fam. So don't be a stranger. Come back and fuck with your boy sometimes."

"I will, fam, believe that."

After we finished giving each other daps, he jumped in a red Escalade that had at least four or five guys in there. They hurried away toward the way the masked men had gone. When I heard the sound of sirens in the background I jumped in my car because I didn't feel like answering any type of questions. Deep down inside I felt like something was wrong, but I really couldn't point my finger on it, and boy was I right? I got word from the streets that Mo got into a bad wreck and there were no survivors. I was so fucked up about the bad news I couldn't stop thinking about it. I knew deep in my heart I never was never going to see Mo ever again.

I was so depressed about what happened and I needed to get away for a couple of hours. I picked up the phone to call D-Black.

"Hello," said D-Black.

"What's good bro?" I didn't wait for him to reply but kept talking. "At nine tonight, I want you and Tu Tank to meet me at Club Phenomenon. I need to get away for a minute."

"Ok, I will pass the word on and see you at nine."

One thing I knew for sure was that I could always count on my family to be there for me.

When I made it to the club, it was super packed. The line was so long it went around the corner. I swear, it was about one hundred people waiting to get in. I could estimate that it was three women for each male that was in the house. That's the number one reason why I love coming to this club, especially on ladies' night. I got out of my car and made my way to the front of the line like a boss. I could tell that the crowd was pissed because they had been waiting in line all this time and here I come making my way to the front. All I could hear was, "What the fuck", "Really", "Who the fuck does he think he is", and "hell nawl". I chuckled a little because that shit was funny as fuck to me I never gave a damn what nobody feels about me, oh hell naw I know nobody is tapping me. I got hot when I felt a tap on my shoulders.

"Nigga, the line is back there," he said, pointing to the edge of the building. "Who the fuck do you think you are trying to cut?"

I looked up at that nigga, ready to smack the shit out of him for the disrespect, but before I even got a chance to raise my hands up, two of the bouncers ran and tacked his ass.

"Nigga, you can't be touching on him like that," said Mean Mugg. "You done lost your damn mind, son."

"Are you ok, King?" asked Terrance, the other bouncer.

"Yea, I'm good," I said. "Y'all made it over here just in time. I was just about to fuck ol boy up."

"I already know," Mean Mugg said. "We are trying to keep the violence down because we already know that you would have the whole club fighting up in here."

I let out a little chuckle and said, "Damn bro, am I that bad? And I'm just trying to stay out of trouble. Let that nigga up, I promise I'm not going to do anything to his ass, he still can come in but make that nigga go straight to the back of the line."

That nigga looked puzzled as fuck over there like I just broke his spirit or something. He's lucky I didn't kick his ass.

"Get the stepping, nigga," said Terrance, as he gave him an extra push to the back of the line.

I looked over and saw this other nigga, he was just staring. I guess that was the other nigga's homie or something. He stared but never said shit. I saw two women standing by him, looking like I hoped it wouldn't be any trouble because I was not trying to get sent to the back. I gave my word that I wasn't going to cause any problems, so I summoned a couple of women to come in with me. And guess what, two of those women that were with that nigga they sent to back, joined me.

I reached into my pocket and pulled out ten one hundred big faces. "Here you go Mean Mugg and Terrance, they are with me," pointing at the eight beautiful women that were behind me.

"Shit, thank you, FAM," said Terrance as he put his money in his pocket.

"King, that's why I fuck with you," said Mean Mugg. "You always keep it one hunda with us."

"It's all about love, FAM, for one, y'all always looking out for me."

"Right on," Mean Mugg, said.

"Come on, ladies, we have a party to attend." I led the way into the club and could tell that the ladies were happy, from all the giggling they did. Shit, it felt like I was big pimping as I had a lady on each arm escorting me inside the club.

"Well ladies, this is where we separate and go our own little way," I said.

"Thank you, Daddy," said this big booty chick, before she gave me a big kiss on my cheek.

As I walked to the bar, I saw my two niggas sitting there, bottle poppin'.

"What's up, bros?" I hollered when I made it to the bar. "How long have y'all been here?"

"We have been here for a while," Tu Tank said, as he waved the bartender over for a bottle of pineapple Cîroc.

"Do you want anything to drink?" D-Black asked me.

"Naw, I'm straight right now, In a few minutes I'm about to go discover the ladies on the dance floor."

"Ok Boss," said D-Black, as he took a sip of his Cîroc.

I didn't see how them niggas could just sip on hard liquor straight. I remembered that one time I tried that, I was fully loaded that I spent about a stack in the club on one dancer. It was so bad my bro had to come to stop me. Those were the good ole days though.

"I'll be right back," I said to them.

"Aiight, we will be right here," said Tu Tank. "If you need us just give us a holla."

When I was making my rounds, I scoped out this brown complexion woman who looked like she was some kind of supermodel. I stopped dead in my tracks, just to admire her beauty to the fullest. She had a small face, a nice high cheekbone structure, and powder pearl hazel eyes with the slightest seductive look like an Egyptian. Even her body appearance was out of control. She had smooth-looking skin, glossy nails, French manicure toes, full-size breasts, and a thin waistline with seductive hips that compliment-ed her pear-shaped butt, dressed in a skin-tight black dress.

Damn, this woman drove me out of my mind, my mind was so messed up I couldn't even think right. I made my way across the crowded room just so I could get her attention.

"Excuse me Ms.," I said. "I couldn't help but notice that you were over here all alone. My name is Kent'e, but people call me King Dreadz and your name is?"

Shorty stopped dancing, turned around with a look on her face that said, whose bothering me this time? She looked me up and down, so I guess she liked what she saw because she shook my hand back``. Her hands were so soft I began to imagine how they would feel, touching my whole body.

"It's nice to meet you, Kent'e. My name is India," she

said.

Damn! India, you just don't know what I'll do to your ass, I said to myself. I guess she was truly feeling a player, because every time she looked at me, I could see the glare in her eyes that read she was thinking the same thing I was. I couldn't help but stare at her. At that very moment, it felt like love at first sight.

"Do you want to go sit at the bar or grab us a table?" I asked.

"It doesn't matter to me. We can go sit at a table," India said, smiling like she just won a million dollars.

I finally got the courage to grab her hand and lead the way to an empty table.

"So, India can you tell me why such a pretty lady as yourself is at a club all by yourself?"

"I am not here by myself," said India.

I began to feel paranoid about everything, wondering if I had come to talk to her while her man was somewhere around.

She must have guessed the cause of the cloud on my face, because she said, "Kent'e, I'm not up here with no man if that's what you are thinking. I came up here with my bestie Strawberry, I don't know where she at but she's up here somewhere."

"So, what you are telling me is that you don't have any type of man in your life, whatsoever?" I asked.

"No, I don't, I just have friends and no, they aren't

friends with benefits. What about you, King? I know you have a special lady in your life."

"Nah, no I don't. I don't have anyone special in my life. I am very single indeed."

I could tell that the lights dimmed down when DVSN "Touch It" music began to play in the background.

I looked at her and she looked at me. I grabbed her hand and led her to the dance floor. We started dancing, our bodies melded together and flowed with the rhythm of the music as if we were making love.

I lowered my hands so I could grip that ass as we danced. I must admit her ass was softer than it looked. I could really get used to this here, damn India what are you doing to me I thought out loud to myself.

After that song went off, the DJ started playing Lah Pat's song, "Rodeo." Everyone in the club got lit when that song came on. After all that dancing we did, we were sweating harder than raindrops. I decided that I had enough dancing for the night, so I walked behind, gripping her waist and leading her back to the table we were sitting at.

India and I talked for half an hour so we could get to know each other better until my boys came over there interrupting me.

"King Dreadz, I need to holla at you for a second," said D-Black.

"What's up, Black?" I inquired, not really liking the interruption and wanting to give India all my attention.

"Sergio called me and said that he really needed to tell you something when you make it home," D-Black said.

When D-Black stopped talking, I introduced him and Tu Tank to India, but as I was doing that, this bowlegged chocolate bone stallion walked up. I must admit her ass was working with something.

"This must be your friend Strawberry," I said.

Strawberry looked lost in thought, wondering what the hell India told us.

"Girl you are a teaser and an eyeball pleaser," Tu Tank said to Strawberry. Strawberry couldn't do anything but laugh at that corny ass joke.

"India, I think it's about time for us to leave because I just received an emergency phone call."

"Okay girl," India said, then turned to me, not really wanting to go. "Kent'e, can I get your number so I can call you up sometimes?"

"Sure, why not! 786-353-7323. Do you promise to call me up?"

"I promise that I will call," India said, as she gave King Dreadz a kiss on his lips. "Bye King!"

"Bye India," I replied, still mesmerized by that sweet passionate kiss.

D-Black looked at me and burst out laughing. "Damn King I didn't know lil momma was working like that bro."

"Say, King, are you going to knock that down?" Tu Tank asked.

"Bro, if you only knew," was all I could say.

"I don't mind taking a bite out of her friend Strawberry, with her juicy ass," Tu Tank said, as he licked his lips, just thinking about her.

All three of us began to laugh at the way Tu Tank was acting. That nigga was a damn fool.

"Damn! I almost forgot. I need to call Sergio up before I forget." I began to dial on my phone.

"Hello," said Sergio when he picked up.

"What's good, bro," I asked.

"I found this dude that has a nice candy shop and he wants to meet up with you."

I really do hate when people go behind my back and have a secret meeting, I thought to myself, because anything could have happened to him.

"If he has a variety type of flavors, I'm down but we will discuss this later," I replied, before hanging up the phone.

Damn, my little brother be pissing me off with shit like this.

When I put my phone back in my pocket, I noticed that the three of us were surrounded by a group of niggas.

"What's up?" I ask, putting up my hands wondering what the hell they wanted.

"I don't like the way y'all was mugging me," said a nigga that was dressed in all black.

"Nigga please," I said, "Nobody was mugging your bitch ass. Get the fuck out here with that bullshit and why the fuck would we be lookin' atcha with all this pussy in the club?"

"Little nigga, I don't like how you are handling me. Keep mouthing off, you are going to find out what I'm about," he said.

"I can't believe this fool is really trying to check me." I giggled out loud. I looked at my boys to see how they were taking all of this in. From being around them for so long, I know that look. It made me know that they were down for whatever.

What really took me by surprise was when I saw two twin brothers make their way to our side. I prayed that they were here to help us. That way it would be five against ten.

"I'm not looking for no trouble," I said. "I promised that I wouldn't fight up in here."

"Plea bargain like a little bitch then," said the man in all black, giving the man next to him some dap.

I wonder if I heard that shit correctly. That nigga had some big balls calling me a bitch. I had a flashback of high school when that nigga Dee called me that. All I saw was red smoke when I stole off on that nigga. My boys and I had the whole club rocking. That nigga tried his hardest to get me, but I sidestepped everything he threw at me. I caught his ass slipping again with a right then left then another right punch, that knocked his ass smooth out. I was on a roll until somebody hit me by the side of my head, with a bottle. I was dazed for a hot second. I looked around trying to see which one of these motherfuckers hit me, but it was really too crowded to find out. Whoever did that shit to me did nothing but pissed me off even more. I went back to work on that nigga but this time I was trying to kill him.

I was still on that nigga ass until I saw that the police were making their way over to us.

"Come on nigga, let's bounce," I said, pointing at cops.

We bust through the crowd so we could go out the back door. I heard the sound of different types of sirens in the distance, and the sound was coming closer to the club.

"Tank, I need you to drive me because I'm leaking out a lot of blood," I said. D-Black jumped in his car and followed behind us.

I looked over and saw that the twins were still riding on our side. I signaled them to follow us because I wanted to thank them in person for helping us back there.

"Do you need to be taken to the hospital, King," asked Tu Tank.

"Naw, take me home," I said, as blood began to drip some more.

I don't know what happened next, because I passed the fuck out. When I woke up, I was lying in a hospital bed, with my head all wrapped up with bandages. I noticed that my boys and the twins were still by my side.

"King, are you ok?" D-Black asked, with concern.

"I'm okay bro. I just feel a little lightheaded that's all. I really appreciate the help back there." Then I turned to the twins. "What are your names?"

"My name is Raymond, and this is my brother Daymond," one of them said.

"It's an honor to meet both of y'all. My name is Kent'e, but everyone calls me King Dreadz."

"We already knew who you are. I wish we could have met you in a better situation," said Daymond.

"Yes, we have heard so much about you," Raymond said. "You are well known in the city and that's why those group of guys wanted to test you out."

"Do you know the nigga that I was fighting with?" asked King Dreadz.

"His name is J.T.," said Raymond. "We know everything about him."

"How would you niggas like a job to join the crew?"

"It would be an honor to be a part of you," Daymond said. "What do we have to do to prove our loyalty to you?"

I gave them a mission that he wanted the brothers to complete. They had to bring me JT's head. It would take them two good two weeks to complete it, but they got the job done.

The doctor finally let me go after running all of those tests on me he told me to make sure I take all of my medication. Hospitals are so freaking boring that's the main reason I never go.

When I made it home, Ki and Sergio were sitting there waiting.

"Are you ok?" Ki asked.

"Damn! I should have been there," Sergio said, slamming his hand on the table.

"I'm ok. Sis, so how long are you going to be here for? I asked.

"I don't think I'm even going back to college. I need to be here with my family," she said.

"OK, sis we will talk later because right now I have a business meeting to attend." She gave me a big hug and told me to be careful.

I met up at a safe spot with Sergio, D-Black, Tu Tank, Daymond, and Raymond.

"Hey niggas, I called all of you to give a vote that would decide if the twins would be joining our organization," I said and looked at my men. "They already showed their loyalty by eliminating the enemy. Those in favor say aye."

"Aye." Everyone agreed that it would be a good thing, so I swore them in and let them know to always stay real within the family.

"Welcome to family," I said. "Your new code names are Gino and Ghino."

I pulled Sergio to the side so I could ask him some questions about that deal. He told me everything I wanted to hear, so I advised him to make the appointment happen. This was a damn good idea, but only time would tell what the future held.

Chapter 13

A Terrifying Encounter

As I was lying there sleeping, the phone began to ring. RRRiiinnnngg!! RRRiiinnnngg!!

Damn, I didn't feel like getting my phone off the charge, better yet, I didn't even feel like getting up at all. My ass wouldn't be feeling like this if I didn't party all night.

RRRiiinnnngg!! *This call better be very important or I'm going the fuck off.* RRRiiinnnngg!!

"Hold on stupid motherfucker, here I come," I screamed at the phone.

"Hello my love, How are you?" It was Tyrone.

What the hell, I groaned inwardly.

"How did you get my new number, Tyrone?"

"You don't have to worry about that, just be glad I

called."

"I don't want you calling me especially with my room-mate staying here," I said, mad that he woke me up. "You are lucky that she ain't here at the moment."

"Why don't you want her to know that we are back together again?" Tyrone asked, trying to sound sad.

"Hold up, we are not together just yet buddy."

"Damn, ok." Tyrone laughed. "Do you have anything special planned for today, Sweetie?"

"I don't know what I'm going to do. It's six o'clock in the morning." I was becoming frustrated already. I just wanted to go back to sleep.

"Well, I guess I will let you go then," he said before he hung up the phone in my face.

Some nerve of this nigga callin' me early in the fucking morning, especially when I was having a dream about King.

As I lay back down, I tried my hardest to fall back to sleep. The only thing I could think about was my new friend King with his sexy ass. I sure hope he wasn't like that last idiot I trusted. Just thinking about him made my skin crawl. But Kent'e didn't seem like he was that type. He seemed passionate, and spontaneous and carried himself well. Just thinking about him made me touch myself, fantasizing that he was making love to me. Immediately, I fell asleep and started dreaming about his sex appeal. He was a tall handsome man I think, about 5'10", long dreads, with the face of an angel, brown skin complexion, and the most beautiful eyes I had ever seen before.

He was dressed to the T in an all-black Stacy Adam suit, white shirt with some gold cufflinks, black and white stripe tie, all-black Stacy Adams shoes, and a dash of red polo cologne. Just the smell of him turned me on. In my dream, I was imagining King feeding me some chocolate-covered strawberries as I lay naked on his bed. We made some good love, the type of love you would only read in a romance book. I woke up from my dream when I heard Irene's loud ass, knocking shit over.

"Damn bitch, do you have to make all that noise?" I threw a pillow at Irene's head.

"Girl, I'm drunk as a motherfucker right now, your ass should have gone to this party. It was the bomb."

Irene kept going on and on about nothing, sounding just like that teacher from The Peanuts. I dozed off on her. I guess she got the picture because I didn't hear her mouth anymore. There I was dreaming again about all the freaky shit I wanted to do to Kent'e.

Damn! How time flies when you are sleeping well. When I woke up, it was 3 p.m. Irene was still knocked out, oh how I wanted to get revenge by waking her ass up. *I'm a let her make it this time but I promise if she ever does that shit again she is going to be sorry that she ever fucked with me.* Some people just don't have respect for others.

I was fully woken and dressed for my Sunday run around the track. Every Sunday, I get up early to prepare myself but today I was late. When I looked in my purse, there Kent'e's number was there right in front of my face. I wanted to pick up my cell phone just to give him a call just to see how he was doing. It was kind of early for me to put any trust in him. I have been hurt so damn much and I wasn't trying to go down that road again. I was nervous, so I decided not to call him.

"If we were meant to be together, God will make a way for us to be together," I said under my breath before tearing up the paper and deleting his number from my phone.

I jogged around the track for a whole hour, damn I was tired, but I kept on walking until I couldn't walk anymore. I could tell that the tone in my legs was showing more from all the jogging I had been doing. Shit, I was tired and I couldn't take another step, so I stopped by the vending machine to purchase myself a red Power Aid. In the background, I could hear someone calling my name.

"India."

I turned around just to see who it was that was calling me. I was surprised to see it was my good friend Strawberry.

"What's up, Lakeisha? I'm surprised to see you here, What have you been up to?"

"I got so much on my mind, so I decided to get out to get some fresh air."

"Girl, I know what you mean with school and all."

"I've been thinking about quitting school these last couple of months, to transfer to a beauty college," said Strawberry. "What do you think I should do?"

"I think you should do whatever makes you happy," I replied. "We are so used to making other people happy instead of ourselves."

"Girl you are so right!"

"Have you given any thought about what you're going to do about your job at Club Sensation?"

"I have given it some thought, Maybe I should keep my job until I finish Beauty College, and then maybe I can open up my own shop."

"That would be a real good idea to look into, that way I can come get my hair whipped up by you. I would love to be your first once you get a shop."

"Aww, you know I got you boo," Strawberry said, as she gave me a big hug.

"I am going to miss all the fun things that we used to do."

"Me too but that's not going to end. Did you ever call that fine gentleman that you were talking to at the club?"

"No, I never did call him," I replied, putting my head down.

"My girl, you are tripping big time. Why not?"

"If it meant for us to be together, we would cross paths again because I believe we all have a soul mate somewhere."

"Girl, I hope you are right."

"I am right I do have a real good feeling about him. I just want to make sure he is the right one for me."

"Oh, ok what are your plans once you are finished with college?"

"I haven't decided yet," I replied, wondering what the future might hold for her.

We held a good conversation for a while until she told me she had to go run some errands.

"Ok Boo talk to you later," I said as I gave her a goodbye hug. I just stared at her as she jumped into her car and drove off. Damn, I wished I could have a tight body like hers. She had that sex appeal down to the T.

When I was walking back to the dorm, I spotted two strange men following behind me. One was fat and the other one was the size of Snoop Dogg. Oh Lord, I hope they ain't trying to kidnap me because my legs are too tight to run.

"Hey Ms., can I talk to you for a minute," said the fat one.

"Hell no, I don't want to talk to you, trying my hardest to run." I wondered what they wanted to talk to me about. I looked behind me to see where they were, damn they are catching up to me big time. Why of all days there's no one around to see what's going on? I tried to scream when they got closer, but this third dude came out of nowhere and stopped me from saying anything. I wondered where the hell he came from and what they wanted from me.

The stranger who grabbed me held a handkerchief with some kind of weird smell, to my mouth. Whatever that shit was knocked me smoothly out. I was sleeping well until someone threw some water in my face. *Fuck, what are they trying to do, drown me?* I couldn't move an inch because they had me tied tight to a chair. I started crying when I looked up and saw the three strange men staring at me with masks on their faces.

"What I did do?" I asked, crying even louder.

They didn't even answer me, they just stared at me. I could tell that I was inside a dark and scary abandoned house, from the smell of the foul odor. It was the worst smell I had ever smelled before.

"Why are you trying to kill me?" I asked, tears running down my face.

One of the men stepped up to me and said, "Where is your boyfriend?"

"I don't have a boyfriend anymore and I haven't talked to him in a long time."

"Don't fucking lie to me," he said, just as he slapped me hard across the face.

"Please don't hurt me, I am telling you the truth. I don't know what you are talking about."

"You know what the fuck I'm talking about bitch," he said with anger.

I began to wonder what kind of shit Tyrone got me in this time.

"Tell me where he is or you are going to be sorry that you didn't."

"I don't know where he is," I said, with my head down praying that they just let me go.

The fat one was about to strike me until the man in the middle stopped him. When I saw what was going on, I flinched.

"Do you think she is lying?" the man on my left asked, talking to the man in the middle.

"I don't know but we are going to be keeping an eye on her to make sure."

After they finished talking to me, they covered my eyes and threw me in a van. When the strange men made a stop, the medium-sized man uncovered my face and told me that if I told anybody about this he would personally have everyone that I love killed. I was so happy as fuck when they let me go on my way. All I could do was thank the Lord for all his blessings because if it wasn't for Him, there was no telling what could have happened to me. I tried to hitchhike me a ride to the hospital so I could get my face checked out, but no one seemed to pay me any attention. They wouldn't even stop for me. Oh, how I wish I could just call the police or my father.

Damn, I thought to myself, I was bound in a fucked-up situation. There was no way in hell I could just put my father in any harm's way if I could call him I would, but they promised to kill everyone I loved. I couldn't wait to make it home so I could soak this sweaty ass body in a nice hot bubble bath. Finally, somebody stopped for me because I don't know how much longer I could have kept on walking. When the car stopped, I ran to the car. It was driven by a woman, who could be no older than seventy-five years old. I could tell she was a Christian woman from all the crosses and Bibles in the car.

"Hi Honey, what happened to your face," said the old lady, as she pulled the door handle to let me in. Once I was in, she handed me some paper towels to wipe my face.

"A couple of dogs were chasing me, so I fell down trying to get away," I lied, trying my hardest not to tell the truth. By the look on her face, she knew I was lying my ass off.

"Oh my honey, do you need to go to the hospital to get your face checked out?"

"Yes ma'am," I said, still trying to clean some of the blood off my face. "I pray that it's not too bad."

On the way to the hospital, the old lady was still asking me a thousand questions about what happened to my face. I'm trying my hardest not to say anything, so I played possum on her so she could leave me alone. I couldn't sleep for shit because this old lady doesn't know how to drive for shit plus I had so much on my mind. I needed to come up with some kind of plan.

Chapter 14

A Risky Business Deal and A Surprising Turn of Events

Three weeks after I met India at the club, I still had not heard from her. I hoped she was okay. I had thought that there might be something different about India, but I guess I was wrong. All women are the same in my book! I can't help to think about her sexy ass though. There was something about her that I couldn't even explain. I could still smell her scent, and picture her innocent face and that tight body of a goddess.

There I was fantasying about making love to her as I sat at the West Texas prison, visiting my uncle. In my mind, I heard India say my name, but it wasn't her at all. When I looked up, it was a guard at the front gate calling my name.

"Mr. Jones, it's time for your visit."

I hurried up and snapped out of that dream. Then I followed the guard to the visitation room. Before she went out of the room, I turned my head to look at that ass once more. *That's a damn shame*, I said to myself, I must admit Shorty was fine as hell.

I hadn't gone to visit my uncle in so long, he probably thought a nigga forgot about his ass. But I didn't, I always sent money, magazines, and books every month. I was also paying the attorney to get him an appeal on his bogus ass case. I wish he were closer to home instead of being way in the middle of nowhere.

I stopped by the vending machine to get two bags of Doritos, two Power Aid drinks, four Kit Kats, and two cheeseburgers. It's crazy we couldn't come in with real money, but only twenty-five dollars' worth of quarters.

I sat there for about two minutes waiting for him to show up. I was just about to get up to ask the guard what was taking my uncle so long when I saw him walk through the door. He was dressed in all white with some kind of brown boots.

"Hey UNC," I said, as I shook his hand.

"What's good nephew?"

"Nothing much, Sorry it took me so long to get back to you."

"Don't worry about that too much, because you are already doing enough for me as it is. How come you didn't bring your brother and sister?"

"I asked them if they wanted to come, but they told me they had something important to do, so I really didn't push the issue too much."

"Oh, ok. Did you know your grandfather came to see me last weekend?"

I shrugged my shoulders. "No, I didn't know he did. I'm surprised he didn't mention it." *I really need to get on my workout game,* I said to myself, because my uncle was looking healthier than I am.

"I been trying to get your case overturned but I haven't heard a word about it lately," I said again.

"Those folks aren't trying to let a nigga go, it feels like they want to keep me locked up in the belly of the beast," my uncle said.

"I promise you UNC. I'm going to get you out of here, one way or another."

"I have faith in you nephew because you are doing all you can to get me out here but if it's the Lord's will, I will be out with no problem."

Who is this man? I never knew him to have faith in the Lord.

We talked for two hours reminiscing about our family until that sexy guard told us that our time was up. Damn time really flies when you are talking and enjoying yourself.

"Well, Unc this was a good visit. I'm a try to come see you next weekend."

"Ok, nephew. Tell everybody that I'm thinking about them."

"OK, I will. Take care of yourself."

When I walked out the door, I looked at the fine officer's name tag. I took out a business card and told Ms. Johnson to make sure she gave me a call one day. I really didn't care if she called or not, India was really the only person I had on my mind. *What the fuck is wrong with me? Kent'e that's not like you.*

I wish I could have had more time to talk to my uncle because he was a great counselor in that love area. As I was driving on the freeway, I started thinking about that meeting I had with my associate, Yun Wun. I remembered that day just like it was yesterday.

"Damn! Y'all niggas still ain't ready to roll yet?" I asked, looking at his gold Rolex.

"We ready to bounce now, Boss," said Gino.

"When we make it to Miami, let me do all the talking."

"Ok, Boss," they all screamed.

I sent D-Black to go get the van with the fake license plates, Sergio to get the duffel bag full of cash and Tu Tank to get the untraceable firearms. Everybody finished what I sent them to do and we got on our way. The estimated time to get to our destination was nineteen hours. That was so much driving.

I have heard so much about Yun Wun being one of the major top players in this dope game, coming from a reputable and wealthy family. He was the Don of the drug Cartels in Columbia, where he had over five thousand soldiers on his payroll. I knew he was a dangerous man that nobody wanted to fuck over.

I really didn't feel right meeting him all the way in Miami, but I had to trust him if I wanted this product. If he tried some funny shit, it was going down like World War II. I was going out like a G. I really didn't want to be caught up in this dope game again, but I needed to make some money, as I didn't want to return to the life of struggling.

I put Yun Wun's address in my navigation system. "D-Black, when we get halfway there, stop at a motel so we can get a couple of rooms to rest because this is going to be a long drive."

I kept looking out the rearview window to ensure we were not being tailgated.

I looked in the back and saw that Sergio, Ghino, Gino, and Tu Tank were already asleep. *Those niggas sleep way more than I do.* Damn, I was happy as fuck when we finally found a motel that had some rooms available, because I was more tired than a mother.

When we woke up the next morning, we stopped at the store so we could get a couple of energy drinks to energize our bodies, because it felt like I had not slept in weeks.

"Damn! I ain't never seen this part of the world before," I said, fascinated.

"It sure does look nice down here," Ghino said, hitting

his twin brother to look.

"Man, look at all these palm trees out here," said Tu-Tank, with excitement.

"This shit right here reminds me of Galveston," said D-Black.

"Hell yeah, it does," I said, agreeing with Black.

We drove around, sightseeing until we finally made it to our destination.

"Man, this is what I'm talking about." I pointed at Yun Wun's three-story mansion.

"This nigga's pad looks just like a big ass castle," said Gino.

"Push the intercom, Black, to let him know we're out here," I instructed.

When the gate opened, four armed dudes came from around the corner with some big ass guns. Tu-Tank picked up his burner, ready to blast anyone who made the wrong move. *What the hell is that little ass gun gonna do, I thought to myself. We really needed to up our game, I realized."

When the gate opened up all the way, one of the armed men waved us to drive through. This mansion looked even bigger up close. Another soldier came out of the mansion to let us know that Yun Wun was inside waiting.

Damn! This nigga gotta have some serious cash to have a baby castle, expensive cars, and a mini army working for him. Yun Wun reminded me of Don Vito Corleone from the Godfather movie.

This place was pimped out with all kinds of exotic things, such as statues, paintings, and antique furniture. Now this was how I wanted to live my life, but I also wanted to be free from the game. This wasn't t the life I wanted to live anymore. The game changed a whole lot, with too many informants and individuals attempting to take your spot.

All that walking around we did in this three-story made me tired. When we made it to the meeting room where Yun Wun was seated, we had to get patted for weapons. They took all our guns and said we could get them back as soon as we left. He had at least four soldiers by his side watching every move we made.

"How is it going, Yun Wun?" I asked as he extended an invitation to shake hands.

"It's a real honor to finally meet the great King Dreadz," he said, shaking my hand back.

What? The great Yun Wun is giving me a compliment I must be doing something right in Texas for him to notice me.

"What can I do for you today, son?"

"I came to do business by buying some supplies so I can re-up on some money."

"How much money did you bring with you?"

"I have at least 140,000 thousand dollars."

"Impressive," Yun Wun said, twisting his goatee

thoughtfully. "That would get you at least 7 kilos of some white ghost. Some of the purest shit from Colombia."

Damn, that's a lot I thought out loud to myself. "That's a deal," I said.

"Hold up son," said Yun Wun, as he whispered something in one of his soldier's ears. His soldier hurried up out of the room so fast.

I *hope everything is ok* I had every kind of thoughts running through my head.

When his soldier came back in the room, he had a big ass duffel bag full of shit. Yun Wun gave him a signal to empty it on the table. Out came some peace pills, red devils, double Dutch, smack, and ecstasy pills.

Damn, this nigga got all kinds of drugs floating around here.

"Do you like what you see, son?" Yun Wun took a puff from his Cuban cigar.

"Hell yeah, I do. I bet you got some of those good killer herbs as well."

"Oh that fire, we keep that in a separate room. Get up and follow me, son."

We walked all the way to the other side of the house. I didn't see any doors anywhere. All I saw was a glass mirror that showed our reflections. When Yun Wun stepped in front of the glass, I couldn't believe what I was seeing. That motherfucker opened up automatically. He had some out-of-this-world high tech in this bitch. I told myself I needed to do a serious makeover on my crib after I made this bread.

Once inside the secret room, there were a lot of pounds of that sticky shit. Never in my life had I ever seen so much dope in my life. That stench was too much I really couldn't even tell the difference between each of them because it hit me all at once. It felt like I just stepped into Bob Marley's personal stash spot.

"Since I like you so much Youngin, I'm a front you 100 pounds of green as well. All I ask of you is to always keep it real with me."

Yun Wun was like the big brother I always wanted. "Yes, big bro. I can handle that."

"If you have a problem with anything, don't be scared to reach out to me."

"OK, I will keep that in mind. We should make it a point to meet up from time to time."

"I will keep that on mind! Is there anything else I can help you with?" he asked.

"No, I'm good. You gave me all that I need, and I really appreciate what you have done for me," I said.

"Well since we are finished with business, follow me so I can show you around the place." Yun Wun led the way, while I followed.

Walking through his castle, it wasn't hard to see that Yun Wun had great taste. In fact, I was ready to copy some of his ideas.

"Well, Yun Wun, it's been a real, big brother, but it's about time for us to head back to Texas," I said when we had come full circle.

"I really enjoyed talking to you, but I have another surprise waiting for you outside." Yun Wun had a mischievous smile on his face.

When we made it outside, I was surprised to see another van, a newer one at that.

"Here you go," said Yun Wun, as he threw me the keys to the new van. Put your goods in this van and use this other one as a detour. Never ever leave in a ride you came in town in. When you're off in these streets you always have to play it safe no matter what."

"Damn! That's deep. I never thought about it like that before. Thanks for the game."

"I already have both vans set up. And the next time you come, make sure you bring somebody to try your products because you don't know if it's sugar or flea powder."

"Flea powder? I asked.

"Meaning, low grade of cocaine."

"Oh, ok I understand what you mean now. At first, I thought you were talking about actual flea powder," I said.

"Lord, I hope nobody would ever buy no cocaine that's really flea powder. That shit can kill someone if they try that shit. Don't ever trust anybody when it comes to your products. I don't give a damn how close y'all are."

"I got you, Yun Wu. I understand everything that I

didn't know before."

We said our goodbyes and got on our way back to the big T. The trip we took to Miami was a real learning experience. We made it out of Miami with no problem, but once we got to Texas that was a different story. In my gut, I had a feeling that someone was tailgating me and my feelings were never wrong. When I looked back, it was a police squad car with no lights on top. As soon as I turned the corner, on came the sirens. *Damn was all I could say.* "Put your hands where I can see it," screamed one of the policemen, with his gun pointed at me.

I applied and put my hands out the window so they could see them. I looked around and there were five new cars loaded with cops, surrounding me. *Lord, have mercy. Is this really necessary?*

"Step out of the car with your hands in the air," another cop said.

I did what they said. I really didn't want to make a scene because these motherfuckers have been killing niggas a lot lately. Every time I look at the news a young black male or female got killed over some bullshit. Nobody really knows the struggles we go through unless the live in our shoes.

***

"I'm relieved I took the decoy van because if I hadn't, I'd be facing some serious federal time. The other van wasn't so lucky. It had all the drugs hidden among boxes of produce, discovered by the authorities on Friday morning. The bust happened after an undercover investigation by Fort Worth officers from the Tarrant County Organized Crime and Narcotics Unit. They had been tailing the van, which had three suspicious men inside. The men bailed out and, despite the cops giving chase, they somehow managed to disappear."

"We still don't have a lead on anything," said Officer Blackman. "We are going to find them and bring them to justice."

I was watching the news and I was pissed. I couldn't believe how much dope and money I just fucked off. I was only glad that nobody got caught at the crime scene. I shrugged off my train of thought, only to realize that I was back in Fort Worth. *Damn, that was a long ass drive from West Texas.*

I pushed the speed dial button to let Sergio know that I was on my way to the house.

"Ok bro, I have some real important shit I need to share with you when you make it," Sergio told me.

"Alright bro, see you in the few, and make sure you call everyone to come to the meeting and tell them to be on time."

"Bet that bro," said Sergio before he hung up.

The journey to Forest Hill took about ten to fifteen

minutes. As I was driving, I was listening to my favorite song, "Tell Me Something Good" by the famous UGK as it came on the radio. It had been a long, long time since I heard this song, so I sang along.

I finally made it to my crib. I hoped that everyone was there already because I really didn't feel like waiting. Whoever did not make it yet was going to get penalized for not handling their business. When I made it to the back of the house, I was surprised to see that everyone was sitting around the table, ready for business.

Chapter 15

Unexpected Reunion and Unwelcome Surprise

Damn! I was still having nightmares about those strange men abducting me. I wondered why they took me and kept me captive when I hadn't done anything I knew of. *Were they looking for someone else that looked like me? Was someone playing some kind of prank on me?* I had a million thoughts running through my head, trying to figure out what was going on, but I wasn't getting anywhere.

I was scared to tell anyone else about what happened because I didn't want anyone to get hurt. Nevertheless, it didn't feel good to have to watch my back every second of the day. Not knowing if I was being followed drove me crazy. I had to lie to Tyrone about why I missed our little dinner date. I used the excuse that my family was having some problems. He already knew how close I was with my family, so he understood everything. I hated lying to him like that, but I hoped his bitch ass didn't stoop that low to have me kidnapped.

A knock on the door startled me out of my thoughts. "Who is it?" I asked as I walked toward the door.

"It's the love of your life," I heard the voice say.

"Naw, for real, who is it? I don't feel like playing any games today. I am picking up my taser." I would be damned if I let anyone else kidnap me again.

"Damn! India, it's me, Tyrone. Why are you so paranoid?"

I looked out the peephole just to make sure that it was Tyrone.

"Well, you know people have been getting kidnapped lately," I said.

"Yeah, I know. We just busted a sex ring the other day—are you going to open the door or what?"

"Oh! Yea, my bad." I quickly opened up the door. There Tyrone was, smiling and looking as good as ever.

"Come in, do you want anything to drink?

"No, I'm good."

When I was putting on makeup Tyrone came behind me and hugged me by the waist. I could tell how close he was by the rise in his pants to let me know how much he missed me.

"I love you so much, India," he said, as he began playing with my hair.

It felt so relaxing as he was rubbing my scalp. It had been a while since a man touched me like that.

I let out a moan, and managed to say, "Let's go, Tyrone or we'll be late for our dinner reservation." I could tell by the look in his eyes that he wanted me bad, really bad. I wanted him as bad as he wanted me, but I had to show my body some self-respect.

Tyrone was being such a good gentleman all night we were out. *I hope he doesn't think he is getting any of this good pussy.* He was going to have to earn some of this killer shit because my milkshake brings all the boys to the yard. After dinner, he decided we should go dancing at this high-scale club. I hadn't been to the club in a good while and it felt so good to be out of the house. It was so live in here I was really feeling the vibe.

I danced for a long ass time that I became tired. I was looking for where to sit my ass down when I noticed him walk in. Damn! I almost fell when I noticed that Kent'e walked in with some more people. I almost forgot how sexy that man was. As soon as he turned around, we made eye contact with one another.

"Hey, stranger," said Kent'e giving me a big hug. Damn! That hug felt so damn good.

I was glad that Tyrone was off somewhere talking to

his friends because he would have had a fit seeing another nigga hugging me.

"How come you never called me?" Kent'e asked.

"I had lost my phone and all my numbers didn't transfer when I got a new phone," I quickly lied to him.

"Oh, ok that's understandable. Let me see your phone so I can put it back in there."

I handed over my phone, so he could give me his number again. I felt guilty that I had to lie to him.

"Here you go, India," he said as he gave back my phone to me. "Please backup all your contacts so you won't lose them this time."

Damn! Kent'e smelled and looked good that night. He was one nigga I wouldn't mind giving some of this Kit Kat. I looked at him and smiled, "Well, how have you been?" I asked.

"I have been living my life one day at a time, trying to survive in this wilderness," Kent'e said.

"I know what you mean. Things haven't been all gravy on my end either," I said, wanting to tell him what happened to me.

"What are you going through that is so bad, India," asked Kent'e.

I looked at him puzzled, just as I started having a flashback about that night.

"Are you ok?" Kent'e asked as he put his hand on my shoulders.

"It's just that I am in my last year of college, and I wonder what the future holds for me," I lied, shrugging away the thoughts of my kidnapping.

I'm not worried about no damn school just my life, I thought to myself.

"I just want you to believe that everything is going to get better for you," Kent'e said. "Life is going to have its ups and downs, but it won't last long. It's up to us to keep fighting the good fight, so don't just give up on life. Keep on moving forward to the future."

Damn! Kent'e was saying some real shit. I enjoyed talking with him. He told me what happened to his parents when he was younger and how he had to grow up to take care of his sister and brother. It was a sad story to hear. I realized then, that he was one strong individual and I felt good about him. He made me feel so warm on the inside from the way he talked and looked at me. It felt like I met this man in another life. *Is this my soul mate or something?* I regretted not keeping it real with him the first time we met. If I did, perhaps, I would be happy now. Damn! I wanted him so bad. I decided that I wouldn't let this man get away again.

"Thank you for the encouragement," I said. "How do you deal with stress every day?"

"I live my life every day like it's my last," Kent'e said.

It was about to get good. I wondered why Kent'e stopped talking and what the hell he was looking at. I turned my head around, so I could see what was going on. There he was, standing behind me mad as hell. *Damn! What the hell am I going to do now?*

Chapter 16

Consequences and Unexpected Alliances

Have you ever had a funny feeling that someone was watching you? I was having that moment. Something deep down inside of me was telling me to turn around to see who was messing with my spirit. I wondered why this big bitch was eyeballing me.

Do I know him?

Do I have some kind of beef with this man?

I had all kinds of crazy thoughts racing through my brain. I knew this nigga didn't want any smoke.

"What the fuck are you looking at pussy ass nigga? asked Kent'e, as he balled his fists.

At that, he rushed my way, ready to rumble. "Why the

fuck are you talking to my girl," he said.

I looked around to see who the fuck he was talking about. I didn't see anyone he could be talking about but what I saw was a crowd beginning to form our way, trying to be nosy. I turned my head back around maybe he wasn't talking to me, and I just took it the wrong way.

"Hold up," I said to myself. He was all up on India. Now, it all came to light. India was the girl he was referring to. I don't know how the hell I missed all of the signs.

"Damn! India, why the fuck you didn't just tell me the damn truth, that you had a fucking nigga," I said. "Now that shit hit the fan, I can see that you didn't lose my fucking number on your phone. You deleted my shit."

"Don't fucking talk to her like that you stupid little prick," said Tyrone, and struck me in my right jaw.

He must have really hit me hard to make me see stars. I was in a daze. I brushed it off and came back to reality. *I know damn well this nigga didn't just put his hands on me,* I thought to myself.

I had to react because I didn't want to look like no pussy in front of everyone. I got up off my ass and start beating the brakes off this nigga. Sergio came out of nowhere and hit that nigga so hard he fell on his face. It sounded like he broke something. I just prayed that Sergio didn't kill him because he did hit the floor kind of hard.

When I looked up there were about five more big motherfuckers making their way across the room so I got ready for whatever was about to happen. What caught me off guard was the presence of the police. I can't stand them pigs because, with them, there isn't any justice in this judicial system, so I know they were either going to kick us out of the club or take us to jail.

So my boys and I dropped our beat-down stance to surrender to the police. After the handcuffs were on, one of these niggas caught me slipping and stole off on me by hitting me in the back of the head.

"Bitch ass nigga, you lucky I have these handcuffs on because I would beat your ass," I said.

Why the hell did the police let that nigga do me like that unless they are friends or something, I wondered. That was very unconstitutional, and I wouldn't treat my worst enemy like that.

About three more uniformed officers made it to where we were and slammed the shit out of us. *How come we are the only ones in handcuffs?*

"They didn't start that fight, it was him," somebody screamed, pointing at India's boyfriend.

"That's not fair. Why are y'all arresting them but not the one who really started the fight," another said.

"We want justice," everyone began to chant. "We want justice. We want justice."

"Shut the fuck up, before y'all go to jail with them," one officer said.

"Naw, fuck you. We know our damn rights," said some

fat man.

People in the club went from zero to one hundred real quick when they started escorting us to the patrol cars. I looked up at India and saw she looked sad as fuck. I could tell she had a lot of regrets. I showed no remorse whatsoever because if it wasn't for that bitch, I wouldn't be in this situation.

"I'm so sorry, Kent'e," India cried out. "I didn't mean to lie to you." Tears ran down her cheeks.

I turned my head away from her because I was disgusted by her presence. As we began to roll out, people inside the club started a riot by breaking shit and chasing those big men off with some pool sticks.

Damn, I wonder how long were we going to be in jail. Please, God, I pray that we don't go to the Mansfield jail because that's one nasty ass place. Semen and all kinds of other shit are on the ground. Somebody really needs to go investigate that place and close it down for good.

"How come y'all didn't take the one that really started the fight, and the one y'all let beat me while I am in handcuffs?" I said, but they didn't say a word back to me.

"Hey, wait a minute, this isn't the way to the Mansfield jail," said D-Black.

"Fuck, these bitch ass laws are about to drop us off on the wrong side of town," I said. There was no justice in this deck of cards we just got dealt tonight, so we just had to go with the flow.

They stopped the patrol cars in the middle of nowhere and told us to get our black asses out of their cars.

"What did we do to deserve this type of treatment?" I asked as the officers began to take off the handcuffs.

The police left us helpless and stranded in the wilderness of an unknown place. Here we were, in this neighborhood, knowing damn well they didn't like outsiders. I prayed to God that he kept his holy hands on us because I have always been a firm believer that he was real. My life has been nothing but by his grace. As we were mopping around, a group of Mexicans approached us.

"Say, y'all are way out of place and there are consequences behind that shit," said a dude, wearing a black shirt.

I looked around and there were a lot of them, but the one who had the black and red hat stood out the most. I guessed that he was their leader, just standing there all calm letting his soldiers handle the situation.

"We are not looking for any trouble," I said. "We are just trying to get back to the house."

"Man, nobody didn't ask you anything," another said.

"Why do people always think that we are some hoes, but this is the wrong time to try to flex."

"We didn't come here for no—" I was saying, but was interrupted rudely.

"Shut the fuck up," he said and pulled out a burner, and put it right in front of my face.

When all of the others saw what was going on, all of them pulled out their burners too for no reason.

"Stop, don't do it," I heard someone say. "I was behind the building when I saw them pigs drop them off dawg. It's fucked up how everyone is treating them when it's not their fault they're in this situation."

"Damn Black Mexican, you always want to put your ten cents in where it doesn't belong," said someone in the background.

"Don't fucking talk to my brother like that," said the one in the red and black hat. "He's right. If they didn't do anything wrong, we shouldn't feel threatened at all, so put them heaters up right fucking now."

They were very obedient to their leader, and no one questioned his authority.

"I'm sorry about this incident," he said, extending his hand for a handshake. "My name is Spook. What's your name, Bro?"

"Everybody calls me King Dreadz," I said, as I took the invitation to shake his hand back.

"So, you are the great King Dreadz? I heard so much about you," said Spook. "I didn't mean no harm to you about this situation."

"I ain't tripping anymore Bruh, just mad that those bitch ass laws left us stranded like that," I replied, even as I thought of a way to get even.

"Wow! I can't believe that the great King Dreadz is in my

face. I heard that you have connections with the Cartel on all the goods."

Damn, the word really does get out. "I fuck with the best of the best drop," I said.

We chopped it up for a hot little second talking about how much the game had changed.

"Here is my info, Bro. Whenever you want to link up and do business, just let me know."

"Thank you," I said to the Black Mexican who spoke up for us.

"No problem, Bruh. I knew who you were when I peeped the laws kicking y'all out of the car. I just didn't want to interfere with them because I didn't want them fucking with me, but I always wanted to be a part of your crew to make some money."

I never knew that some of these people thought I was some kind of legend. That nigga saved my life, so I owed him. That nigga and I hit it off big time, so we decided to let him be down with the family with his big bro blessings. Forming alliances with others was always a good thing.

Chapter 17

CHAPTER 17
INDIA CHEYENNE

Torn Between Two

I tried and tried calling Kent'e, but he never answered any of my calls. I even left messages on his voicemail, to apologize for what happened.

Sigh! I don't blame him for being mad at me, I know I fucked up big time. I wish he would call me just to let me know that he was okay.

"Kent'e, it's me again. Please call me. I would love to work out our problem," I said into the phone for the umpteenth time. I was desperate at this point. "Bye, hope to hear your sweet voice soon."

I didn't know why the Lord was always making me go through all these trials and tribulations all the time. I just had not seen anyone go through so much shit as I had. Just once in my life, I wished that things would be in my favor. The more and more I thought about my life, the sadder I got. So, I got down on my knees to say a little prayer.

Dear Lord, I'm down on my knees, coming to you in prayer to ask you to forgive me for all my sins. I know that there isn't anyone perfect in this world that we live in, but Lord, it gets hard sometimes, living in this world, not knowing the unknown. I know deep in my heart that you have someone that's my soul mate, that's already created, just for me.

Tears rolled down my eyes, as I felt a deep longing inside of me. I just wanted to be happy—my number one fear was growing old with no one to love me. When I got done praying, I hurried up so I could use the bathroom. I had to pee so badly that my stomach started cramping.

When I got back from the bathroom, I realized I had been in there too long as I had so many missed calls on my phone. I went through all my messages hoping I had a message from Kent'e but felt sad that there wasn't any. They were only calls from Tyrone. I realized then that I needed to move on since there was no miracle of Kent'e getting back to me. So, I called Tyrone back.

"Hello, Tyrone," I said. "How are you?

"Hey, India. I'm doing okay. How about yourself—What are you doing?"

"I'm doing ok. Just over here chilling, trying to get my mind in check. I wish I were over there, so you keep me warm," I replied.

"I wish you were over here as well, so I could hold you close to my heart," said Tyrone.

"I miss you being inside me." I purred as my imagination went wild. "Do you want me to come over there, Tyrone?"

"Yes, dear," Tyrone said.

"Wear something sexy for me." I moaned.

"Okay," he said real fast, before hanging up.

I loved Tyrone but deep down inside, I wanted to be with Kent'e.

When I made it to Tyrone's house, he didn't do any talking whatsoever. He caressed my face with his strong dark brown hands. He was being so romantic, trying to take me at ease. *Is this the same person I knew from the beginning of the school year, I wondered.*

"India, you know that I love you right?" Tyrone kissed my neck, trailing kisses down to my cleavage.

"Yes, I know you do." I moaned, squirming from side to side, enjoying the moment.

"I think it's about time that we take our relationship to the next level," Tyrone said, as he got down on his knees and took out a fat diamond ring.

I had never in my life ever seen a ring as big as this one, besides the ones celebrities give to their spouses.

"India, would you do me the honor of being my wife?"

"Yes, I would be delighted to," I squealed, as tears rolled down my eyes. God heard my prayers so quickly. Dang!

The ring was so big I couldn't raise my hand.

Although I accepted his proposal, my heart still felt reluctance as I pondered the situation in my head. *I hope I know what I'm doing by accepting his proposal again because I'm not trying to get my feelings hurt like I did the last time.*

That night we made love like never before. Still, while Tyrone was hitting on that cookie, I was fantasizing about Kent'e being the one. I just couldn't help it.

"Owww fuck, this dick is really good," I said, dripping wet.

"This is daddy's pussy," Tyrone said while nutting all inside of me.

We had sex two times that night and both times it was Kent'e I saw. Damn! I wanted that man badly.

The next morning, I woke up tangled in the bedsheets, a mix of emotions flooding my mind. I couldn't shake off the lingering image of Kent'e, his presence haunting my thoughts. As I lay there, my hand subconsciously reached for my phone on the nightstand, hoping against hope that there would be a missed call or a message from him. But once again, disappointment settled in as I realized there was nothing.

Tyrone, still fast asleep beside me, stirred slightly, his arm loosely draped over my waist. I watched him for a moment, his peaceful expression masking the whirlwind of confusion within me. A pang of guilt tugged at my heart as I contemplated the events of the previous night. I had accepted his proposal, pledging my love and commitment, yet my heart remained entangled in a web spun by another man.

Quietly slipping out of bed, I tiptoed to the bathroom, my mind craving a moment of solitude amidst the chaos of my emotions. As I splashed cold water on my face, I looked at my reflection in the mirror, searching for answers. The tears that had fallen in the depths of the night still lingered in my eyes, a visual reminder of the inner battles I fought.

Chapter 18

Love & Deception

*D*amn, that bitch is bugging me. She left me a shitload of messages. Was I wrong for not answering any of her calls? Hell naw, if it wasn't for her, I wouldn't have got into any trouble at the club.

I honestly did like her a lot because she was different, and I never met anyone like her before. How I wish that the circumstances were different instead of all the lies that I endured.

I still couldn't believe she played me like a fool, making me think that she didn't have a boyfriend. I would have given her the whole world just so she could be happy.

But what was my excuse for not telling her who I really was? It was hard to tell someone you are a notorious drug *dealer and a stone-cold killer. What real female would want to be with someone like me?*

It would be best for me just to leave her alone and don't drag her into my madness.

People always told me that everything happens for a reason. I did like her, but she played me like Willie Foo Foo. Besides, I didn't want her to be a part of this lifestyle.

I need a ride-or-die chick, who's going to suck this dick real good with no strings attached.

I was so deep in my thoughts and didn't see when Ki walked into the study.

"What's wrong with you, big brother," asked Ki, as she sat next to me. "I can always tell when something is on your mind."

There is nothing wrong with me, sis," I said, knowing damn well that I was hurt. I didn't want any of my family to know that I was weak when it came to loving a person.

"Why does it look like you just lost someone that you truly loved?" Ki didn't let it go.

"I'm not looking sad."

"Yes, you are nigga. I saw that same look growing up when we lost our parents."

Damn, she just won't give up, I sighed to myself.

"Ok damn," I started. "I'm going to tell you because you ain't going to let this shit go. I met a chick that I can honestly say I was vibing with, but Shorty wasn't keeping it real with me. She had a whole boyfriend that I didn't even know about."

"Maybe she had a good reason to put you on the back burner," Ki said. "She probably was weighing out her options, because she wasn't getting the love, she deserved with him."

"Huh, I never thought it that way," I said, my words dripping with sarcasm.

"Fuckk, you, Kent'e."Ki playfully hit me in the arm.

"Brother, there is something I would like to talk to you about." Ki's face took on a whole serious look. "I want to start going with you on those business trips."

"You can't be serious." I chuckled.

"Yes, I am. You don't think I can fucking handle myself or something," Ki said in anger.

"I just wouldn't be able to live with myself if anything happened to you," I replied.

"I know how to take care of myself, brother."

"I already know all that—I'm just saying."

"Kent'e, you already running around like the mafia, so I know I'm well protected," Ki pleaded.

"We are some untamed gorillas that won't stay in no cage." I laughed out loud. "I guess, Ki just listen to everything I say."

"I will, brother. I promise," Ki said, as she hugged me. " Have you come up with a name yet?"

"Yes, I did," I replied, smiling. "The M.O.B Cryme Family."

"Oh, okay catchy. So what does the M.O.B stand for?" Ki asked.

"Money Orient Ballers," I replied. That had a good ring to it, so I decided to roll with it.

"I like that brother—we are the M.O.B Cryme Family, so give us our respect or get dealt with." Ki sounded so excited.

From then on we were not to be fucked with. When mothafuckers knew about me, they knew about that M.O.B Cryme Family as well. Damn, I didn't know if shit was about to change for better or worse, but what I do know is I need to prepare myself.

Chapter 19

A Night To Remember

It has been five months since I was engaged to Tyrone and things have been better for us. We haven't set down to come up with our wedding date just yet, but I couldn't wait until that day when I would settle down and have some kids. It still seemed as if my life wasn't complete just yet, because being alone was not fun at all.

I looked at the dress I just got hanging in my wardrobe. I was going to wear it this evening because my best friend decided to throw me an early bachelorette party. I couldn't wait to see how it turned out.

Ring! RRRiinng! RRRiiinnnngg! I picked up the phone.

"Hello," I said.

"What's up sexy?" I heard a deep voice say.

"Who is this?" I asked, *knowing damn well I knew who this is*, as a smile lit up my face.

"It's the man of your dreams."

"Naw, who is this for real?" I asked, giggling like a schoolgirl.

"It's me your Prince charming, Tyrone, the love of your life."

We both laughed.

"Hey, baby, what's up?" I asked.

"Nothing much, just sitting here getting ready to leave," said Tyrone.

"Where are you going?" I asked.

"Well, sweet cakes, I have a function that I have to attend in Los Angeles."

"How long are you going to be gone for?"

"About three days tops, no longer than that, I hope. I wish I could come play in that pussy, but Daddy doesn't have no time."

Hmmmmn. "I love when you play in this pussy Daddy, you always keep it moist and warm."

"Baby you need to stop talking like that before I come over and miss my trip," said Tyrone.

"No baby, don't do that I know how important this trip is for you so go."

"Ok baby, I'm about to head on out. I love you," said Tyrone.

"I love you too, Tyrone, and stay out of trouble."

"I will, bye."

"Bye, baby." I hung up the call, as the smile lingered on my face. I loved Tyrone, even when I couldn't stop thinking about Kent'e.

RRRIIINNNNGG... RRIIINNGG.

My thoughts about Kent'e were interrupted by another buzz from my phone. I was a bit irritated, as I wanted to be left alone to fantasize about Kent'e.

RRIIINNNNG...

I searched for my phone as I had dropped it after Tyrone's call. *Found it!*

"Hello, Irene," I said as soon as I received the call.

"What's up bitch, are you ready yet?" she asked.

"Hell yeah, I'm dressed and ready for this night. Bitch I'm looking the shit, and I'm ready to shake this ass," I replied.

"No, you didn't." Irene began to laugh. "Oh well, I am ready for us to make this a night to remember."

"Girl, I feel you on that. Let's get it poppin," I quipped.

Irene came to pick me up in a Bentley limo a few hours later. It was nice. I didn't even know they made them. Together, we had a couple of shots of Jack Daniels. While we drank, we talked and laughed about our men. When we finally made it to the club, I was already wasted.

The driver got out to open our door. "Have a really enjoyable time ladies," he said.

"Damn, he's kind of cute," said Irene.

She was drunk as fuck, and I couldn't help but laugh.

You could tell it was ladies' night by how packed it was over there in the club. Irene and I had VIP treatment as we were let in immediately, going past a long line of people looking to get in.

I could tell that them bitches didn't like that one bit.

I heard someone mumble, "*What makes them hoes so damn special?*" Another one said, "*I will snatch the weave off them bitches' head.*"

"Oh, try me. I really wanted to beat some bitches up for the disrespect," I murmured under my breath. Anyways, I wasn't about to let them dumb bitches ruin my night, so I let it go.

Inside the club, we were having a lot of fun watching the male strippers shake their dick in our faces. There were some wild broads up in here. They were putting money in the thongs of these male strippers and doing it with their mouths. I *couldn't do any shit like that,* I thought, watching them.

I looked up and this light was shining down on me.

"There is a special request for Mrs. India," the DJ said. "Congrats on your future, let's make this a night to re-member."

I almost wet my pants when he started playing the *Genuwine Song "Pony."* This dark brown-skinned man came out on the stage dancing. He made it to where I was and started stripping right in front of me. I was so embarrassed I didn't know what to do. All I heard was women screaming, *"Take it off Daddy, take it off."* So he started taking off the rest of his clothes. He was built like a black Arnold Schwarzenegger. I damn near wet my panties when I rubbed my hand on his chest and trailed it down the rest of his body. Everywhere was hard as steel. *I could get used to this*, I thought.

I took my eyes down to see his manhood. I was shocked and thrilled at the same time. This nigga's dick hung like a horse. It dawned on me how he got the name *Black Stallion*.

I was glad that the show was over because I couldn't take it anymore. My pussy walls were tightened with all that nerves getting excited.

"Damn, India. Did you see the size of that dick?" Irene asked.

"Hell, yeah." I rolled my eyes, ready to get the fuck out of there.

"I would fuck the shit out of that nigga," Irene said, drooling over the stripper.

"Bitch, you are crazy," I said. "He isn't about to stretch this pussy out."

Suddenly, this female walked by and bumped me. I almost lost my balance and looking at her, it was obvious that she did it deliberately.

"Bitch, watch where you are going," I said.

She turned and looked at me with disdain. "I got your, bitch—tramp." Then she slapped me hard across the face.

Without thinking twice, I picked up a bottle and hit the bitch, song "Hit That Bitch *With a Bottle"* played in my head, although I couldn't even remember who sang it.

I looked up and there was blood everywhere. *What just happened?* She was on the floor, her eyes closed, in the pool of her own blood.

"Oh my God, I hope I didn't kill her," I said, already crying.

Everyone stared at me.

"Come on, girl. Let's get the hell out of here," Irene said and pulled me by the hand.

We got the fuck out of that club so fast. In the distance, I heard the wail of the police siren and the ambulance. We made it to the limo, and I was in deep shock the whole ride to my house.

"It wasn't your fault," Irene said, comforting me.

I still didn't say one word. I just couldn't believe what just happened.

"Well, I'm a spend the night with you girlfriend so we can talk when you are ready to," said Irene.

This night was one of the worst nights of my life. All that blood on her face made my stomach hurt. I had never been through anything like that before. I tossed in bed, thinking and wishing I could turn back the hands of time. I wished that I had ignored her. It was only later that I was able to close my eyes and have a wink of sleep.

The morning sunlight pierced through the curtains, illuminating the room and stirring me from my uneasy slumber. As my eyes adjusted to the light, the memories of last night came rushing back, filling me with a mixture of shock and regret. The events at the club replayed in my mind like a horror movie and the weight of what had transpired settled heavily upon my shoulders.

I turned to see Irene, my loyal and supportive friend, still asleep beside me. The sight of her peaceful face provided a glimmer of solace in the midst of the chaos that had unfolded. I knew I could confide in her when I was ready, but for now, I needed to process everything on my own.

Guilt gnawed at my conscience as I questioned my actions. How did a night that was supposed to be about celebrating my upcoming marriage turn into a violent altercation? That slap I received had triggered something within me, an instinctive reflex that had spiraled out of control. I never imagined myself capable of such a violent act, and the consequences were now staring me in the face.

I reached for my phone, hesitant to confront the aftermath of my impulsive actions. The news would surely be abuzz with reports of the incident. It took a moment to gather the courage, but eventually, I opened a news app and searched for any mention of the nightclub altercation.

There it was, a headline that sent shivers down my spine. "Violence Erupts at Local Nightclub, Woman Critically

Injured." The pit of my stomach churned as I read the details of the incident. The woman I had struck was in critical condition, fighting for her life. The weight of the consequences crashed down upon me, and tears welled up in my eyes.

Regret washed over me like a tidal wave. I never wanted this to happen. I had allowed my anger and impulsiveness to consume me, and now someone's life hung in the balance. I couldn't bear the thought of being responsible for such pain and suffering.

At that moment, I realized the importance of taking responsibility for my actions. I had to face the consequences of my choices, whatever they may be. But first, I needed to find a way to help the injured woman, to make amends for the harm I had caused.

With a heavy heart, I turned to Irene, gently waking her from her slumber. As her eyes fluttered open, she sensed the turmoil within me. Without needing to say a word, she knew something was gravely wrong.

"Irene, we need to do something," I choked out, my voice trembling with remorse. "We have to find a way to help that woman, to make things right."

Irene, her expression filled with empathy, nodded in understanding. "You're right, India. We can't ignore what happened. We'll find a way to make amends, to ensure justice is served. But we also need to take care of ourselves and seek legal counsel. We can't let this consume us."

I clung to her words, finding solace in the promise of finding a path to redemption. Together, we would face the consequences of that fateful night, own up to our actions, and do everything in our power to make things right.

As we embarked on this daunting journey, I knew it would be a test of my character and resilience. The events of that night had shattered the illusion of a carefree existence, and now I had to confront the darkness that resided within me. It was a painful lesson, but one that I vowed to learn from and use as fuel for growth and self-reflection.

Little did I know that this incident would serve as a turning point, not only in my life but in the lives of those around me. The path to redemption would be a long and arduous one, but I was determined to face it head-on, seeking forgiveness and seeking to become a better version of myself.

And so, with a heavy heart and newfound resolve, I embarked on a journey of self-discovery, understanding that true growth comes from acknowledging our mistakes, seeking amends, and finding the strength to rise above the darkness that threatens to consume us.

Chapter 20

Flame James Album Release Party

It was the day of the album release party for Flame James. I always loved that country rap tunes sound, from songs such as *"Yellow Tape," "What That Is,"* and *"Last Year."* It was a real honor to get some invitations from Flame.

I knew for sure that my goons and I would be the best dressed at the event because, besides my grandfather Macedonia, there wasn't anyone else on our level. Speaking of my grandfather, I hadn't seen him in a while.

I called my goons to see if they were ready to roll out because the two stretch limos were parked outside.

Well, I was dressed and ready to do my damn thing. I

looked sharp from head to toe. There was not a day that I didn't look fly anyway. I looked in the mirror and I was satisfied with what I saw, I sprayed on some of my designer cologne —the one that always impressed the ladies.

Everyone finally arrived and we were ready to leave, so we could have a good time. Ki, Sergio, and D Black rode with me, while Ghino, Gino, Tu Tank, and Black Mexican rode in the other limo.

The limo had so many drinks and snacks to choose from. I drank so much alcohol from the limo bar that I was already drunk as fuck before we even got to the event.

We finally made it to Flame James party and it was hella packed. I already knew that nigga was going to rock the crowd tonight with his bangers.

Once, we were in the building, I spotted a whole lot of celebrities that I knew.

I was peeping the scene out when I spotted one of the baddest chicks in there. She had a dark skin complexion, a thin waist with some seductive hips, an apple-shaped booty, thick in the thighs, standing about 5'4. She had long sister-loc hair with honey-blonde highlights. Shorty had it going on for real, so I had to introduce myself to her.

"Excuse me, Ms. can I holla at you for a second?" My mouth dropped to the floor when I saw who it was. It was none other than the video vixen named *The Dream Catcher*, in the flesh.

I had to come up with something quick if I wanted to

pull her. "Hi, my name is Kent'e but people call me King Dreadz and I wanted to come over to get to know you."

"You don't know who I am," said Dream Catcher.

"No, I do not, but I would love to," King Dreadz lied, trying to play it cool.

"My name is Jasmine Dixon, but people know me by the name, *The Dream Catcher but you can call me Jazzi*. I have been featured in a couple of music videos and magazines. Here is my number, Kent'e, Make sure you give me a call sometime."

"I sure will," I replied.

Man, I swear tonight is the night I still can't believe that she gave me her number.

RRIINNG. My phone began to ring. I picked up immediately because I had been waiting for the call.

"Hello. Do you have that information I was looking for?" I asked and listened for a while. "OK, I will be there in a minute."

Chapter 21

CHAPTER 21
INOIA CHEVENNE

Ain't Nothing Change

I had so much fun at my bachelorette party until the fatal incident involving that bitch and me. Even though I still couldn't sleep, I came to the realization that there was no need for me to feel guilty because that bitch had it coming.

Now that I think about it, I realized she was the one talking shit when we were going into the club talking all that shit about snatching some weaves off our heads.

I don't fuck with nobody, and I be damn if I let a motherfucker fuck with me so stay in your lane bitch, I thought, clenching and unclenching my fist.

After making coffee for myself, I thought of my mother.

I had not spoken to her in a while. So, I dialed her number.

"Hey Mommie, how are you," I said, happy to be on the phone with her. "I'm sorry that I haven't been calling you as I should. There has been so much going on in my life that I needed to sort out because you made me a strong independent woman."

"I have been so worried about you my sweet baby," my mother said. "You could have at least called me to let me know that you were ok."

"I know—I'm sorry, Mommy," I said.

"Your cousin Jameka is back in town, and she asked about you," my mother said.

"How long has she been back?" I asked.

"It's been about three days now," my mother said. "I told her that you moved to Texas. Honey let me tell you that girl has really changed a lot. Remember how skinny that girl was in high school? Not now, child, she did put on some weight."

"Yes, Mommy I do. I remember it just like it was yesterday." I went down memory lane to the conversation I had with Jameka.

"Jameka what are your plans when you get out of high school," I asked.

"I'm going to be one of those top-notch hoes that's going to be getting that bread for real," Jameka replied. "Them niggas going to have to bring their A-game for real, if they want a taste of this pussy."

"Girl, you are so crazy." I had laughed it off.

"Shit, pussy is the ruler of all things," Jameka said, sounding like she was some kind of scholar or something. "India, you know niggas will do any and everything to get a shot of this pussy. That means giving you money, cars, and whatever else they have to give."

"Ha Ha Ha Jameka, you need to write yourself a book called The Pussy Monster 101," I told her.

Damn, those were the good ole days that me and my cousin had. I shrugged off those memories.

My mom was still rambling on about something, and I knew she could go on and on if I didn't stop her. "Ok Mommy, I have to get ready for my doctor's appointment. So please give Jameka my number and tell her to call me."

"Ok baby, I will," said my mother. "I pray that I hear from you soon."

"You will. I promise. Take care and I love you."

"I love you too," my mother said before hanging up the phone.

It took a while before I saw the doctor and I was glad when I was finally done. I went home and just wanted to have a relaxing bath. After my bath, I checked my phone and saw that I had several missed calls. Two were from an unknown caller, while five were from Tyrone and one from Irene checking on me.

The first message said, "Baby I know you see me calling." It was Tyrone. "Give me a call when you get this message."

The next message was from Irene. "India, I'm just calling to make sure you are doing okay. Make sure you call me back."

The next message was from an unknown number. "Hi cousin, this is Jameka. I guess you might be busy or something. You can reach me at 404-555-4502, Hope to hear from you soon, bye."

I hated that I missed Jameka's call because I didn't want her to think that I was trying to be funny. So, I reached out to her immediately.

"Hi, you have reached Jameka. I'm not in at the moment so if you would leave your name and number, I will be sure to return your call back at my earliest convenience. Have a nice day and God blessed you." Beep!

"Hey girlie, this is India. I was just giving you a callback. Sorry, I missed your call earlier. I was taking a hot relaxing bath. Call me when you get a chance."

Later that evening, my cousin hit me up. We didn't talk that long but I did give her my address so she could hit me up when she came to town. I couldn't wait to catch up with her because it seemed like she did grow up some.

One night I decided that I wanted to watch a scary movie alone with my scary ass. I was so deep in the movie when I heard a loud noise at my door. That scared the shit out of me that it made me drop my popcorn all over the floor.

"Who is it?" I asked, trying my hardest to look out the

peephole. I couldn't see a thing because whoever it was held their hands against the peephole.

I really didn't feel like playing any games that night. I must admit that I was scared as fuck, not knowing if it was the same dudes that held me captive a while back.

"I'm on the phone with the police right now and they are listening to everything I'm telling you, so if you don't leave right now, they are on their way," I lied, knowing damn well I didn't want to go back down that road again.

Whoever was on the other end realized that I wasn't playing and removed their hands from the peephole. Oh, shit, it was my big-headed ass cousin playing games.

I opened the door. "Girl I'm gonna kill you if you ever do something like that again. You scared the shit out of me."

"I'm so sorry cuz," Jameka said laughing. "I didn't mean to scare you like that. I would have kept playing but I didn't want the police to come taking me to jail. What kind of trouble are you into girl?"

"I'm not in no trouble," I lied. "Why would you ask me that?"

"It was the tone in your voice. You sounded kind of edgy that's all," said Jameka.

"Girl, come give your cousin a hug," I said, changing the subject.

"Damn, it's been a long-time cousin since we have seen each other," said Jameka.

"I know huh! Would you like anything to drink? I

have cranberry juice, Diet Coke, water, and Kool-Aid. You know black folks have to keep them some Kool-Aid."

Jameka started laughing. "Girl, ain't that the truth but I will take a diet coke, please. I have to keep this figure looking good."

"So what have you been up to?" I asked as I served her the drink.

"I really haven't been doing anything spectacular just been trying to get my life in order. I'm so tired of being an exotic dancer," said Jameka, as she took a sip of her diet coke.

"An exotic dancer?" I asked in surprise.

"Yes, girl. I became one in my very first year of college," Jameka said. "Don't get me wrong I get paid a whole lot of money, but the men can be pricks. They will call you all kinds of names if you don't want to have sex with them. "They are like, *Bitch you think you're all that, I didn't want to fuck your stinky pussy anyway,*" It is so frustrating.

"Wow! I never knew how obnoxious some men are."

"Girl I know!"

"Did you ever do anything that you regret?" India asked. "Be for real on this matter. I promise I won't judge you."

Jameka looked at me all sideways for asking a question like that. "Hell no, I'm not a hoe if that's what you're thinking. I never gave up my pussy for money. I had this one man in my life that I was so in love with, and he broke my heart by sleeping with two of my friends."

"I'm so sorry to hear that."

"I thought I had everything," Jameka said, as tears flowed freely. "I gave that nigga my all, and he couldn't even love me. I didn't even care about the money just his love."

"Where did you meet him?" I asked.

"I met him when I was working at the Magic City strip club. In the beginning, he was so different from all the other fellas that I had been with. He showed me so many good times telling me that I don't ever have to worry about nothing in the world."

"Aww—he sounded so sweet," I said.

"He insisted I stopped working at the strip club just to make him happy, but he stopped appreciating all the things I did for him."

"It's going to be okay." I patted my cousin on the back.

"Enough of that mushy shit," Jameka said, looking calm as ever. "What have you been up to cousin?"

"Well not too much of nothing," I said, showing off the big ass rock on my finger. "I'm engaged to be married."

"Congratulations, cuz, I'm happy for you," Jameka said.

"Thanks! But my mind is kind of twisted right now." *I was sure I had a confused look on my face because I felt the confusion creeping up on me.*

"What's wrong?" asked Jameka. "You can open up to me."

"I love him dearly, but I keep on thinking about another man," said India.

"Damn, how did that happen?" asked Jameka, wanting all the juice.

"Well, it all started when I met this man. He was such a gentleman but to make a long story short, I never told him that I had a boyfriend at the time. My fiancé Tyrone and I were having problems seeing eye to eye on some things."

"Don't get me wrong—he was a good man, but he stayed jealous, he was a cheater, and he never paid attention to my needs," I continued.

"How can you get engaged with someone knowing that you are in love with another man?" Jameka asked curiously.

"People have been doing this since the beginning of time," I said, shrugging. "This other man was so mad at me for not telling him about Tyrone. When we were at the club, they had one big fight and ended up going to jail."

"Wow!" Jameka's eyes widened in shock.

"I know that's messed up, but I didn't mean for that to happen that way. But now he doesn't want to answer any of my calls."

"Do you blame him? I wouldn't have answered any of your calls either," said Jameka—"better yet I would have blocked your ass?"

What the hell? She didn't just say that to me. This is the wrong time to be playing games with me or I am going to smack the shit out of her ass, I was thinking this while looking at her.

Before I could say anything else, Tyrone walked in.

"Good evening, ladies,* said Tyrone.

Hi, baby." I went to him and planted a kiss on him. "Jameka, this is my handsome fiancé I was telling you about."

"Hi, Ms. Jameka, it's a pleasure meeting you," Tyrone said, as he kissed her hand.

"Ok—so are y'all hungry? I said.

"Yes, I am," Jameka said. "I haven't had any real good food in a long time."

For the rest of the night Jameka and I sat around talking and eating Chinese food, laughing about the good ole times. Jameka didn't have nowhere else to go so I let her stay here for the rest of the time she would be in town. Nevertheless, for some reason, I felt like something was wrong, but I brushed it off by saying that I was just being paranoid.

The next morning, I woke up bright and early, so I could go work out at the gym and run a few errands. I left a note on my bed, saying that I would be back later, and to call me if they needed anything. I kissed Tyrone on the forehead before I headed out.

My day went in a breeze. Later on, that evening I couldn't believe how energized I was. I swear, that was one of the best workouts I ever had and on top of that I got all of my errands done with no problems whatsoever. I decided I couldn't wait to put my feet up and relax with

Tyrone and Jameka, and some wine.

When I walked into the house, all I could hear was moaning. *Damn, Tyrone why do you have the TV turned up so loud,* I thought as I walked deeper and deeper down the hall. I followed the sound because it became louder, and sounded like it was coming from my bedroom. Just then, I heard the words, *"Give it to me Daddy."*

Slowly, I reached out my hand and pushed the door open. My heart dropped at the sight that was in front of me.

Chapter 22

A Night of Chaos: Unintended Consequences

Man, it was really fucked up that my nigga Red Rum got murdered. I never thought that there would be a day I would be going to another funeral. Being at this funeral made me think about how my parents got murdered for no reason. I can't believe they never found the ones that were responsible for their deaths, I swear on my life that I would take revenge when I do.

Every time I looked at the news a celebrity had died. There was Tupac, Aaliyah, Left Eye, Whitney Houston, Michael Jackson, Bernie Mack, and my nigga Pimp C—all gone. On the day I found out that Pimp had passed away, my whole life turned upside down. What is this world coming to? There was so much pain and stress living in this world.

When word got back to me on who murdered Red Rum, I called a meeting that night.

"I have called this meeting because I am my brother's keeper. As you know one of our own got killed a couple of days ago," I said to my men.

"That's fucked up how they did him," Gino said.

"What are we going to do about this situation King?" D-Black asked.

"I received information on the ones that committed this crime. It was two niggas that goes by the name Solo and Tristan. I heard they were some certified head bustas that's about their business."

"We are going to bring them niggas to justice tonight," I said. "I'mma take Sergio, Tu Tank, and Gino with me on this mission. Black and Ghino, I want y'all to hold down the fort for me until I return."

"Ok, Boss. I got you," D-Black said.

As we were riding, I sat and thought about all the wrongs I did in my life. It was about time I changed it to something positive. However, until then, I'mma continue being Judge Dredd and I would serve justice on the two fuckers who murdered Red.

"Okay, stop right here," I said. "We don't want to go too far down. We don't want to make a really bad scene, just do what we came to do—nothing extra. My source told me that they are out here every night at the same time."

"Sergio, I want you to go around the corner to peep and see if they are still outside," I directed.

"Ok, bro, I'm on it," replied Sergio as he went to peep.

"What's the word, Bro?" I asked.

"Yeah, I saw them on the porch with some more niggas strapped up," replied Sergio.

"Ok if anybody gets in the way they are going to feel the wrath of the M.O.B Cryme Family," I said to my soldiers, as I prepped them for war.

"Tu Tank I want you to stay in the car," I instructed.

"Ok, Boss!" Not only is Tu Tank the number one hammer for the family, but he is also the best driver.

As soon as we got out of the car, we ran to one corner so we could catch them slipping. I looked around to make sure everything was good to go.

I pulled out my burner.

"Oh shit, Gino said. "There goes some pigs coming creeping from around the corner with their spotlights on, and they spotted us."

My heart dropped when I saw them smash on the gas to catch up with us. When Sergio saw what was going on, that nigga took off like a trap star with that big ass AK47 still in his hand. When the two laws saw Sergio run, they jumped out of their patrol car to chase him but ran right past Gino and me as if we were some ghosts or something. And the funny thing about the situation we still had guns in our hands.

Gino and I hurried up to the whip where Tu Tank had been waiting.

"Damn," Tu Tank said. "Where the fuck did those laws come from."

"I don't even know. Let's dip to drop these guns off somewhere and then come back for them later."

"We drove until we found a secure place. All I could hear was sirens in the background. I prayed to God that Sergio got away okay, but deep down inside I felt something totally different.

"Let's get out and go check on Serg," I said and turned to look at Gino. I could tell that nigga was scared shitless. I was scared as well because I really didn't know what to expect. We left the car where it would be safe and ran back to where we once were. I couldn't believe my eyes when I saw all the police cars, ambulances, and fire trucks. All I could hear was a lot of screaming.

'Help. Help. Bro help me," said Sergio screaming in pain.

"Them pigs broke my brother's leg by hitting him with that damn police car," I said, trying to make my way over there. "Let me go nigga, let me go."

But Tu Tank wouldn't let me go.

"Fuck!" Sergio cried louder.

By this time, the whole neighborhood was outside trying to be nosey. You know how Black folks get when there is commotion going on especially if it has something to do with the police.

"Why did y'all have to run over that man like that?" asked one neighbor.

"It's none of your damn business," said one police officer.

I can't believe how these laws think they can just hide behind their badges, but if you catch them alone somewhere I bet, they will catch that Jack Mack.

"You don't have to be so damn rude," said another neighbor.

"Do any one of y'all motherfuckers want to go to jail?" asked an officer of the law.

"What are you going to take us to jail for—we ain't did shit," said the nosey neighbor.

"Fuck you, we ain't going anywhere," said Tu Tank

"We know our fucking rights."

That law was for real. He really was going to take us to jail. A black and a white officer started making their way over to us so we decided to run back to the car. If it wasn't for all those other laws and nosey neighbors, we could have murk him and got away with it.

On the way back to the house, I had to tell the family the bad news.

"Is Sergio going to be okay?" Ki asked, crying hell of loud in my ear.

"We don't know yet," said Tu Tank.

"What happened," D Black asked looking worried as hell.

"Just know we were at the right place at the wrong time," I said.

Now I had to be the one to tell Gramps the bad news. I filled Gramps in on the whole ordeal on what happened.

"Don't worry grandson," said Gramps. "I will get Mr. Howell on this right away."

I tried to go to sleep but I couldn't. All I could think about was my brother lying down on that dirty ass ground, crying in Pain. All kinds of crazy thoughts were running through my head.

Tonight was just not our night, I mumbled to myself as I shook my head.

Chapter 23

Betrayals, Apologies and Regrets

A m I dreaming or something? Please, Lord, tell me that I'm dreaming.

I felt so betrayed and disgusted at the same time. I couldn't believe that I just caught Tyrone and Jameka having sex on my bed.

"Bitch, how could you do this to me?" I asked. "I took you in when you didn't have anywhere else to go."

"Let me explain, India," said Jameka, as she tried to put her clothes back on. "I didn't mean for this to happen."

I just stood there in rage, ready to go strike her when she put on her clothes halfway, because I'm not up for no discussing, period.

"Baby! Baby! I'm so sorry," Tyrone said. "Let me explain

what happened." He just laid on the bed, still naked.

"Really nigga? You just going to go there with me when I gave you my all and this is the thanks I get, Tyrone. So don't baby me, because you've been messing up ever since we met."

I was so enraged by everything that I rushed at Jameka and began choking her.

"India, you are hurting me," Jameka cried.

"Bitch I don't give a fuck. You didn't care about me when you slept with my man," I said as I kept on swinging, not giving a fuck where I hit her.

"Baby that's enough," said Tyrone, as he jumped up trying to break up the fight. The only way he succeeded was because he was way bigger than I am.

'Let me go Tyrone you have no right to put your hands on me," I yelled, trying my hardest to get away by clawing him in the chest.

"Are you going to calm the fuck down, if not I can keep you like this all night" Tyrone said?

"Yes, I'm going to calm down," I lied, but in my mind, I had a plan as soon as he let me go.

Tyrone let me go and I immediately hit him in the eye. It must have hurt because my hand hurt.

"Damn India," Tyrone said. "You hit me in my eye. What the fuck is wrong with you?"

I started hitting him some more because I wanted him to feel what I felt—PAIN.

"How does that feel? I asked and then hit him in the nose. Blood began to pour all over my floor.

"Fuck," said Tyrone. "You are crazy. I never seen this side of you before."

I continued attacking him and hit his nut sack. He fell to the ground in serious pain.

"Ok, I'm tired of this shit," Tyrone said and managed to stand up and knock me to the ground.

I hit that floor pretty hard because I felt it on the right side of my hips. I couldn't do anything but look at both of them while tears began to pour out of my eyes.

"I want both of y'all to get out of my house right now," I said, as I struggled to get up.

"Please no, India. I don't have anywhere else to go I'm truly sorry, so can you please find it in your heart to forgive me? I never meant for any of this to happen."

"Bitch, if y'all don't get out my house, I promise I'm going to kill the both of you," said India.

I guess they thought I was bluffing or something because they both stood there. I was done talking. I jumped up and went to my dresser drawer, where I kept my new nine-millimeter handgun.

When they saw what was in my hand, they both bolted out of my bedroom and out the front door. Tyrone was so scared that he didn't even try to cover up his naked body. I ran behind them with my gun, just to scare them, but what they didn't know was I didn't have any bullets loaded in this gun. I surely wasn't going to tell them because I wanted them to feel the hurt and shame I did. Now they knew that I wasn't playing any games.

Hahaha look at the both of them running like some cowards, I thought to myself.

When they looked back and saw that I was still on their tail pointing my gun, they hurried up and jumped in Tyrone's car.

I still couldn't believe they were having sex in my bed. I blamed myself for being so trusting. I shouldn't have left both of them here by themselves. I never knew they would be this trifling and do me like this. I gave up Kent'e, to be with Tyrone, for what? Kent'e was mad at me and probably would never speak to me again. I decided that if I ever got the chance to talk to him, I would apologize, for not keeping it real with him.

I was so distraught that I called Irene and told her everything that happened at my place.

There was a long pause on the phone.

"What did you say? Irene asked after recovering from the shock. "I'm not even surprised that happened. You must have forgotten that your cousin was one of the biggest hoes in high school. Everyone knew that."

"I know she was, but I thought she changed."

"Well, obviously, she did not. Rule number one—never ever leave any chick around your man especially alone.

"Yeah, I know." My head dropped in pain. "I thought

I could trust them. I didn't think it would go down like this."

"I'm sorry that you had to experience something like this, but I told you about Tyrone from the beginning."

"I should have taken your advice and not talked to him because he always seems to hurt my heart every time I give in to him."

"Take my advice, BFF. Drop him and find you someone else who's going to cherish you because you deserve better."

"Amen to that, because I'm so tired of all this heartache."

"I love you, India, and hey if you ever have anything on your mind, don't be scared to reach out to me."

"I love you too best friend," I said before I hung up.

That night I tried to go to sleep but I tossed and turned until the wee hours of the morning.

The next morning I felt a little better but I still felt like shit because I couldn't sleep. I couldn't take my mind off Tyrone. So, I did the one thing every woman did to get over heartbreak—shop!

One thing I didn't like about Texas was how small the mall was. The only mall I really enjoyed was the Grapevine Mills Mall, which had a lot of stores to choose from.

As I was walking around shopping, I spotted Kent'e with a new woman on his arms. I felt so sad deep inside, seeing him like that. Now I fully understood why he never answered any of my calls nor called me back. I couldn't really blame him though, because I was the one who didn't keep it real with him, so he moved on to some other chick.

Even though he was in a relationship now, I still needed to tell him how truly sorry I was that he had to go through something like that.

"Hey Kent'e, how are you?" I asked.

"Hey, I'm doing good! How about you?"

"Well, to tell you the truth it's been hard," I replied. It wasn't the time to be emotional, but I fought to keep the tears at bay.

"Excuse my manners—Jazzi this is India, India this is Jazzi."

"Nice to meet you," I said. I really didn't want to shake this girl's hand especially if she was my competition.

"Nice to meet you as well," Jazzi said.

"Kent'e, I need to speak to you in private," I said.

"Here baby," King Dreadz said, giving Jas a thousand dollars in cash to go shopping. "Go buy you something nice and let me handle this right quick."

"Ok baby," said Jazzi as she gave King a nice big kiss on the lips.

She did that shit on purpose, oh how I wanted to reach out and beat the shit out of her.

"What's up India? It looks like you have a lot on your mind," King Dreads said, looking at me intently.

Tears began to flow, I tried to wipe them off, but more came.

"Talk to me, I'm all ears."

"I would like to start off by apologizing to you Kent'e," I said in between sobs. "Tyrone and I were going through some hot mess at the time, and I really didn't know what I wanted. And when you came into my life I was blown away and I wanted that feeling to last a lifetime, so I want to be honest with you. I didn't lose your number, I deleted it from my phone because I was confused."

"I knew that you erased my info," said King Dreadz. "Well not really, I didn't know until I had that scratch with your boyfriend."

"I'm so sorry I didn't mean for none of that to happen. I made a huge mistake—the man I thought I loved, cheated on me with my cousin."

"Wow, I'm so sorry to hear that." Kent'e comforted me.

"That's what I get for treating you like I did."

"No don't think that way, Things happen, and that doesn't make it right to get cheated on."

"I know, but it made me realize that I wanted you in my life," I said. "Every day I thought about you. When I made love to him, it was you I was thinking of."

"Wow, I don't know what to say," said King Dreadz, just as Jas began walking towards us. "I'm so sorry for what you had to deal with, but I have a lot of things to think about."

"Ok, thanks for listening to me." I hugged him.

"Take care, India," said King Dreadz, as he met up with Jazzi.

"Bye, Kent'e." waving him goodbye.

Kent'e didn't say if he forgave me or not. It was a loss I wasn't willing to come to terms with.

Lord if you can hear me can you please open up Kent'e eyes to let him know that I really do need him in my life because I feel that you made him just for me. I can't live with myself if I let him get away, India prayed, In Jesus' name Amen!

Chapter 24

Struggles of The Heart

It was really good seeing India. I didn't even know that I would bump into her as I did but I could sense that Jazzi was upset with me for letting her shop by herself so that I could talk to India. She didn't even say one word to me on our way back to my spot. Once inside the house, all hell broke loose.

"So King, what type of relationship do you have with that woman in the mall," asked Jazzi, ready for an answer.

Oh, Lord, I knew it was coming I just didn't know when.

"Baby, please don't start—she ain't anything but a friend. I told her that if she needs an ear to listen I'm here no matter what."

"Hmm! If you say so," Jazzi said with a smirk on her face.

"I can't tell she's just a friend from how she was looking at you. I know women and I know that look, did you have sex with her don't lie."

Wow! This is crazy, I thought to myself. Women always have to find something to pick at a man about. If you are doing wrong, they are fussing. If you are doing good, they still find something to complain about, we can't win for shit.

"What look was that? "I asked, knowing damn well I knew what she was talking about. Since talking to India, she expressed to me what I meant to her. I must admit I was wrong for not accepting her apology. I just wanted her to suffer awhile so she could take me seriously. I didn't have time to play any games with anyone.

"Don't play no games with me, King," said Jazzi hitting me in the arm. "You know you noticed that look as well as I did."

"Come here Jazzi," I said. "You know you are the only woman that I want in my life."

"Aw, honey, you are so sweet you are the only man that I want, you complete me," said Jazzi as she gave me a big passionate kiss on the lips.

"Damn! I almost forgot how sweet these kisses were," I said, pulling Jazzi closer to me.

"You like that huh," said Jazzi playfully sucking on my tongue, as we kissed.

"You know I do," I said, enjoying every moment of it.

"Well, follow me, and let me show you how much you mean to me." Jazzi guided me to the couch.

I followed her lead because every wish was her command. I was excited to see what was going to happen next. As I sat there on the couch, Jazzi started slow dancing for me, at a very slow seductive dance. The way she moved reminded me of a snake. She made me want to get up off the couch, bend her over, and give her the business.

We didn't get to have sex as often as we liked because Jazzi was always out of town on business. Being a celebrity comes with a whole lot of responsibilities. Her fans loved her so much that they are getting her face tattooed on their bodies. I never could understand why fans do that.

Jazzi and I might not have the perfect relationship, but I would do any and everything for her, because she deserved the moon, stars, and everything else that comes along with it.

When I finally snapped out of my thoughts, I noticed that Jazzi was fully naked, with her chocolate Coke bottle figure that every girl wished they had.

"Come here baby," I said. She obeyed my every word and came to me.

When she approached me, I gripped her and then smacked that fat ass because I loved how it jiggled when I did it. Damn this girl looked so damn good I just wanted to taste every inch of her body. As she danced in my lap, I noticed that my big black stick began to rise, so I felt her soft perky boobs. I couldn't believe how soft her skin was, it reminded me of a newborn baby. I really didn't want this day to end. I would love for it to last forever but reality said it couldn't.

Before it got to the good part, my phone rang so I stopped what I was doing to answer it.

"Hello," I said, frustrated that his dance had been interrupted.

"You have a collect call from Michael Jones an inmate at the Robertson Unit. To accept this free call press one, to refuse this call, hang up, or press 2." the operator said.

Pushes number one on the phone.

"Hey Unc," I said, as I got up to go somewhere private to talk. I tried my hardest to keep this side of me hidden from people outside my circle.

"What's up with you nephew? asked Uncle Mike.

"Man, if you only knew half of it," I said.

"Word on the street is that your brother Sergio is on lock in the county," said Uncle Mike.

"Yeah, a little situation happened, and he got hit by a patrol car when he took off running."

"Damn, that's cold. How is he doing?" asked Uncle Mike, concerned about his nephew's well-being.

"He's fine, the hospital had to put some metal screws in his leg, because they shattered his bones." I wished that night never happened.

"Why is he still in that place, asked Uncle Mike, do y'all

have a lawyer?

"We are waiting on Mr. Howell to find the officers who did this so we could work out something."

"I hope that everything gets taken care of," said Uncle Mike.

"It will Unc, Don't worry everything will be okay."

"Ok nephew, stay up and remember to stay focused because time is precious," said Uncle Mike.

"I will Unc. In a few weeks, I will be up there." *Man, how I wish that my uncle was out right now because I know everything would be taken care of. I hate having the world on my shoulders.*

"Ok nephew," said Uncle. "The phone is about to hang up. Stay safe."

"I will, Unc. Keep your head up as well." I hung up.

When I went back into the living room where I left Jazzi, I noticed that she wasn't in there anymore. She left me a note stating that she had to be in Miami to do a photo shoot with this top magazine company called Big Booties. I never heard of that company before. Now that she was gone, I didn't know what to do to occupy the time. Damn! My uncle had to call at the wrong time. Now I was sexually frustrated. I really hadn't been myself with everything going on around me.

I have been having so much on my mind lately and it seemed like my spirit and soul were fighting one another every day. I wanted to change my life around, but I didn't know how to because I am nothing but a killer and a drug dealer, so who in their right mind would ever love me for me and not for my money? Did love even exist? Is it real or is it a figment of our imagination? Love vs. deception is what we face in this world. It was like we were stuck in the matrix. The only woman I knew who had truly loved me was my mom.

The sound of the doorbell got me out of my train of thought. *"I wonder who that could be,"* I thought aloud to myself. When I finally made it to the door, I looked through the peephole and saw a familiar face staring at the door.

No, it can't be, I couldn't believe what I was seeing! Was I dreaming or did I die and go to Heaven? Well, I know I'm not in Heaven so I must be dreaming it's not real. I opened the door to see if I was imagining this moment.

"Hi," said the woman, as she gave me a big comfy hug.

Acknowledgements

I would like to thank my CREATOR for all His wonderful works and blessings He has bestowed upon and within me. Without His love and guidance, I couldn't have finished this book. Thank you for granting me this blessing and helping me realize that I am not special, just blessed.

I am blessed and thankful to have such a wonderful mother (Debbie). You are my backbone, and without your love and support, I don't know what I would have done with my life. Just know I love you dearly.

Angel, thank you for making me feel wanted all the time. You are one of the best little sisters a big brother could have. I wouldn't trade you for anything in the world.

Flame James, thanks for always having my back and never giving up on me when I was at the worst point in my life. Just know that I am my "Brother's Keeper." I am proud of you, Bro.

Neka, thanks for supporting me in everything I do

with your crazy self.

VaKeisha Hill Robinson, thanks for always riding for me by keeping the haters in check behind your big bro.

Lil Vic, thanks for keeping me on my toes when I was slacking.

My sisters Kenya Crosby and Kenequa love y'all!

Kamry and Cythnia, I am so proud to have daughters like y'all. I want you to know that you mean the world to me, and I thank the CREATOR for making you.

To my nephews, Dajorian (DJ), Damarion (Mon Mon), James (Baby James), Keith (Keke), Rylan, and my nieces Jordan, Aliaha, and great niece Nova, your uncle loves you dearly.

To Artemus "Auto" Harris, my music partner in crime, thanks for being a true friend.

My Southern King Family, J. Real & Ken Dawg, I can't forget about my day one fam.

Demarcus and Mark Anthony Wallace my little brothers from another mother thanks for pushing me and being some of my best supporters.

I want to thank my Editor, Queenbee Aurora, for taking my novel to another level. I can't wait to see what you have in store for other books.

To my day one, my brother from another mother, Keith Barnett, we have been tight since the beginning of time.

Turkessa White, From the moment our paths crossed, my life has been illuminated by your love and unwavering support. You have been my rock, my confidant, and my greatest cheerleader through every high and low. Thank you for being the heart that understands my silence and the soul that fills my days with joy. I am profoundly grateful for your unwavering love and steadfast support. With you, I've found a love that is timeless and true.

Jasmine your inspiration has breathed life into the new second character in my book, and I couldn't have asked for a better person. Thank you for sharing your essence with me.

Shay, you've been there from the very beginning of this process, guiding me through every step of my book-writing journey. I'm incredibly grateful for your presence. Our history is deeper than the ocean.

Janisa Van Dyke thank you for taking the time out to help me get this book right, even though I know I get on your nerves sometimes. lol.ly appreciate that! Monica Van Dyke, Sereda Van Dyke- Shird, and Kenneth Coles thank yall for taking me in by treating me like family I am forever grateful.

A special shout out to everyone that's a part of my

life in no particular order I love all of yall: Quesha, Jea'nine, Shun, Rechanda Woods, Kammicakes, Quamaine, Kemond, Mahoghany, Ebony, Josiah, Ricky, Mika, Monique, Loc By Ria, Recka, my bestie Natalie Anzai, Jasmine Coleman, Annette Nicole, Mom Renee, Shamae and Tay Tay Harden, Brittney Lusk Brown, Iceyess, niece DJ, sis Nikkie Pooh, niece Dejaa Jackson, Dre Lockett, Tony Lockett, Highlife Lil Keith, Jarvis Glenn, AC Moses, RED, AD Muhamad, Phyleise Herndon, Aunt Tomeka, Aunt Bev & Uncle Ford, Aunt Pat & Uncle Carl, Aunt Cynthia, Aunt Mary, Aunt Bonita & Uncle Blue, Aunt Bonnie, Equria, TT, Tasha, Candice, Carlena, Tyrone Jr, Aunt Sandra, Aunt Tonya, Aunt Floria, David, Stacy Brunswick, Bunkie, Black, Lil Kevin, MoMo, Chandler, Jessica, Christina, Dwaine Nichols, Frankie Smith Nichols, Pastor Brown, Taryn, Fannie Lee (Grandmother), Uncle Mike, Uncle Waymon, Uncle Alex, Lil Terry, Brittney Stolden, Lil Bonnie, Shavon Brazier, big cousin Vince, Lil Vince, Lil Kevin Stolden Jr, Lil Mama, Wayne, Binky, Quack, Kphill, Donyell, Edward, Lil Malcolm, Kesha Lynne, Cousin Alex, Camellia, Marco, Naitai, Paul, Nelda, Cousin Ray, Ray Barron, Ryan Rhodes, Shalanda, Sharesha Williams, Tracy Wallace, Adrienne, Deray, Lin Butta, Frances and Jasmine, Waymon Smith, Dawn, Mia, LaTonia, Lakiesha Marrow, Greg, Net Washington, Jo Jo, Shun, Shae, e2three, Lucy, Daryl, Robert, Don, Buck, Lil Robert, Chris, Curry family, Wallace-Davis family, Aunt Alma, Mercedes, Johnny, Twilla, Lil Britt, Mashia, Zee, Alica, Alisha, Roosevelt, Dimplz, Kandice, Carolyn, Tasha, Tammie, Ashley, Tony Burks, Terrance Jones, Jessica Jones and family. In loving memories to my other father Deacon James Harden Sr, Uncle Kenneth, Rodo, Sherri Hill, Kevin Stolden Sr, T.i.p Lil Pula, N.i.p Lil Pat & Kurt, Carla aka Lady

About the Author

D on Hendrixx is a Fort Worth, Texas native who showed an interest in the arts at a very young age. In fact, it was through music, poetry, and short literary stories that he found not only solace but inspiration.

His interest in music culminated with him becoming a founder of the regionally noted rap group "Southern Kingz Finest."

Don is now embarking on a new career in authoring and is expected by many to emerge as a standout author in a new generation of powerful literary storytellers.

While not being busy crafting his next bestseller, Don Hendrix enjoys spending time with family, indulging in a wide range of music and literary works, learning new things, reflecting on life, and offering love and friendship to his loved ones and members of his local community.

Afterword

The Connection Between Love & Deception:

1. Deceptive Love: Some individuals may use deception to create the appearance of "love" or "affection" for personal gain, such as financial support or emotional manipulation.

2. Jealousy and Insecurity: In romantic relationships, feelings of jealousy and insecurity can lead to deception, as individuals may hide their true emotions or actions out of fear of losing their partner's love.

3. Betrayal: Deception can be a form of betrayal in which one person violates the trust and love of another by lying or engaging in deceitful behavior.

4. Protecting Loved Ones: Some people may resort to deception in order to protect their loved ones from harm or to spare them from the truth, be-

lieving that it's an act of love.

5. Self-Deception: Individuals may deceive themselves about their own feelings of love, especially
   in cases of unrequited love or when they are in
   denial about the true nature of a relationship.

It's important to note that while love and deception can
be intertwined, honesty and trust are typically considered
crucial components of healthy, meaningful relationships.
Deception can erode trust and lead to the breakdown of
love, so maintaining open and honest communication is
often essential for the sustainability of love in any relationship.

www.ingramcontent.com/pod-product-compliance
Lightning Source LLC
Chambersburg PA
CBHW060312260626
47160CB00007B/2580